Caroline – who can do the splits and who could have been a world famous ballerina

...in ...publishing and magazines. Despite that, she worked in publishing for fourteen years before starting to write her own books. She has had nearly forty books published, for children and adults, and is also the editor of various educational magazines. Caroline lives in Kent with her two children, two cats and two dogs.

Cherry Whytock,

the illustrator of *Cringe!*, lives in an old Kentish farmhouse with a large fluffy cat, a dog, a husband and two grown-up daughters (who actually only come home when Cherry is cooking something spectacular, i.e. not very often). Her hobbies are gardening and buying face creams. She sometimes paints pictures and has an ever increasing collection of shoes.

Cherry – who makes necklaces out of her old earrings and who definitely can't do the splits

CRINGE!

CAROLINE
PLAISTED
&
CHERRY
WHYTOCK

MACMILLAN CHILDREN'S BOOKS

First published 2003 by Macmillan Children's Books
a division of Macmillan Publishers Limited
20 New Wharf Road, London N1 9RR
Basingstoke and Oxford
www.panmacmillan.com

Associated companies throughout the world

ISBN 0 330 41558 1

5 7 9 8 6

A CIP catalogue record for this book is available from
the British Library.

Printed and bound in Great Britain by Mackays of Chatham plc, Kent

For Julie Simpson

Julie Simpson
Who has really long legs

CONTENTS

TELLING IT HOW IT IS

This is my book. This is Amaryllis Rosanna Lillian Flowerdew's private book. Any member of my family caught reading this book, including and especially my repulsive younger brother Hugo, will drop dead INSTANTLY!

Anyway. I need to start at the beginning.

OK. So I am thirteen. OK – so I am very nearly thirteen. I live at home in London with my family, the Flowerdews. Yawn, yawn.

I am the only girl (well, I suppose there is my mum as well but she doesn't really count).

I have TWO brothers. Why did I get such bad luck? Pity me. I don't know which is the most disgusting of my brothers so I will start with Ben.

Ben is sixteen. He left school last term and told everyone that he had become a Street Poet. I don't really know

1

Amaryllis – me,
total babe

Total
Babe

Hugo –
smarty-pants
know-all.
Particularly
keen on
scientific
experiments

Mum –
counsellor, works
from home

Dad –
runs a health
food shop

what a Street Poet does, but I think it's probably got something to do with graffiti. Ben isn't his real name. His real name is Geoffrey. He was named after some bloke called Geoffrey Chaucer who wrote these really weird poems called The Canterbury Tales — something to do with Canterbury in Kent, I suppose. But the poems are dead boring and don't even rhyme. Geoffrey is a real nerd's name so I'm not surprised that he's changed it.

Ben lives in the cellar of our house. It's really creepy down there. All dark and spooky because there are no windows. I've only been down there once.

Ben thinks it's great. Or at least I assume he does because Ben doesn't really talk to anyone. He kind of grunts at people instead. It would probably have been better if he'd changed his name to Grunt instead of Ben.

Whatever, Ben lives in the cellar. He doesn't seem to care about the dark — but then he's asleep most of the time, anyway. If he isn't asleep, he's hardly ever at home because he's always slipping out of the coal hole from the cellar and straight into the street to go off with his mates. Ben's got this band. It's called GOB. Mum thinks GOB stands for Get Out of Bed. Obviously my mother is extremely dumb.

I've heard GOB play. They are pants. Not at all like a proper boyband. But there is this really fit guitarist in the band called Jake. He is GORGEOUS and I think he is in love with me. If he isn't now, I'm sure he will be when I am thirteen.

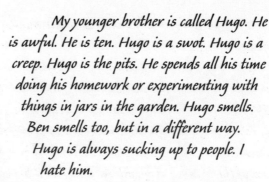

My younger brother is called Hugo. He is awful. He is ten. Hugo is a swot. Hugo is a creep. Hugo is the pits. He spends all his time doing his homework or experimenting with things in jars in the garden. Hugo smells. Ben smells too, but in a different way. Hugo is always sucking up to people. I hate him.

Now, my mum and dad are really weird. They are not like any of my friends' parents. Thinking about it, I am not surprised that Ben and Hugo are so peculiar because they have Mum and Dad as parents. What I don't understand is how they managed to have me? I think I must have been adopted. Or found on the doorstep. Or perhaps I was swapped at the hospital for their own baby by mistake? Mum and Dad won't admit it but I think something like that must have happened because I am the only normal person around here. I am the only one who likes to eat Coco Pops, drink Coke and watch telly. (Which I have to do at Nono's — that's what we call my gran — because we are not allowed to have a telly here. Dad

6

says it is because 'a telly would close our minds to artistic things'. Perlease!)

My mum is called Mary and she is extremely old. She was forty-two on her last birthday! And she TOLD EVERYONE!! My mum is something called a Counsellor but it isn't anything to do with houses. She says she Helps People to Find Themselves. Shame she hasn't helped Ben find his way out of the cellar in daylight. Anyway, all these people who need to find things come to our house and Mum talks to them on the sofa. She's put a sofa in Ben's old bedroom and she sits there with these people talking for hours. Sometimes I wonder what they are talking about. But not often.

When Mum isn't doing that, she is writing poetry. She thinks she is really cool at it and she belongs to this thing called Circle of Poets. She goes off with them once a week on Wednesday nights and they read each other the poems they've written. Mum dragged me off to one of their meetings once because she said I'd enjoy it. They all clapped when Mum read out her poem. I thought the poem was pants. It was like so embarrassing.

But my dad is even more embarrassing than Mum. His name is Marcus and he is always saying that we should call him Marcus instead of Dad. I don't know anyone who calls their dad by his real name. Anyway,

my dad has this really embarrassing shop. It's called
FLOWERDEW AND SONS AND DAUGHTER. It's a health-
food shop but none of the stuff he sells in it smells good or
tastes remotely healthy to me. Even school dinners taste better

than some of the stuff he's got in there. Dad wears sandals without socks all year round. He even comes to meetings at school in them. It is so embarrassing! Nono knits Dad lots of jumpers out of scraps of wool she finds.

Frank, a parrot with a past and a very fruity vocabulary

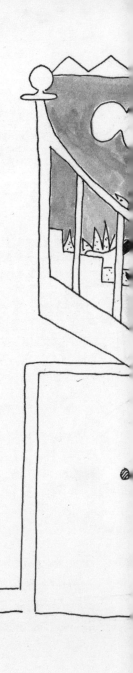

Dad keeps a parrot at the shop. He's called Frank and he was given to Dad by some old man who used to live in our street. The man used to be a sailor. Frank's really cool because he swears all the time. Dad gets really stressy with Frank when he swears at the customers!

My dad reckons that he is an Artist. He goes to something called Life Classes every week. But I don't think much life goes on there. Nono says he paints ladies' bits and pieces – what does she mean by that? He's certainly painted a woman with lots of wobbly bits on the wall going up our stairs!

I don't know what Mum's people think of it when they go upstairs to sit on the sofa and find their inner selves.

Brian, ultra cool ex-greyhound, shares Nono's sherry

Nono, often wears pale blue and sme deliciously of hyacinths? freshly baked bread

I've already mentioned Nono. Like I say, she's my gran and, as grans go, she's quite cool really. She looks just like a granny should. She's got bluey-grey hair and she has it 'done' at the hairdresser's every Thursday on what they call Twilight Day (that's the day they do it cheap for pensioners). Once a week, Nono has her Baking Day. I love it. She makes these delicious gigantic cakes and puddings. Nono never, never, ever

12

makes things with mince or chicken though. She never makes you eat liver or anything else disgusting like that. I don't think Nono ever makes savoury food. Like I said, Nono is a proper granny. She's called Nono because she starts almost every sentence with the words, 'No, no'.

I go and see Nono on my own after school sometimes. Well, quite a lot really. This is because:

☆ there is always something good to eat there

☆ Nono is the only other person I know who really seems to understand how impossible my family is

and

☆ Nono lets me watch the telly

Nono has a dog called Brian. He is a retired greyhound and all he ever does is lie around on Nono's sofa looking elegant and graceful. Brian is nothing like our dog. Our dog is called Giggles but he never looks like he'd be able to laugh. In fact, Giggles is extremely bad tempered and sits and sulks in the corner all the time.

Sometimes I watch those ads on the television — the ones for dog food or loo rolls. You see these really cute dogs that bounce up to the

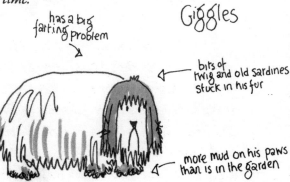

Giggles

has a big farting problem

bits of twig and old sardines stuck in his fur

more mud on his paws than is in the garden

people in the adverts and look pleased to see them. Giggles never speaks to anyone and he SMELLS. Dad expects me to take him out for a walk but it is just not on. Nono asks me to take Brian out for a walk but she pays me to do it. This is useful because it's the only pocket money I get. Dad says that pocket money is just bribery. How would he know? He never gives any!

Xanthe, on the other hand (she's my best friend), gets loads of pocket money from her mum and dad. She has what's called an allowance. Sometimes she's got so much money she has some left over to put in her bank account.

I haven't got a bank account. All I've got is a mouldy old Post Office book I was given by Nono when I was born.

Xanthe is beautiful. She has long, black hair and great, big, dark eyes with enormously long eye lashes. They are so long she doesn't even need to wear mascara to school.

Xanthe's mum is the business. Unlike my mum she is not old and she is slim and wears fabby clothes. She looks like a model and she runs her own business making exotic Indian jewellery. Xanthe's dad is a barrister and he earns POTS of money wearing a suit. They live in this gorgeous house which is always being written about in magazines. They go on holiday every winter and every summer. They never go camping like we have to. And they never have to go off to celebrate the Solstice. Why did Xanthe get the parents I should have had?

So, that's me and my cringeworthy family. I suppose I haven't said much about me, have I? But this book is all about me so I will say about me in the rest of it. Meantime, here is my self portrait:

moi!

And this is what I am going to look like soon:

DISASTER!

I've already explained that my mum goes to this thing called Circle of Poets. She goes along and sits in the community hall listening to all these pencil cases reciting their diphthongs and stanzas (whatever they are). But this evening she did something terrible and said I had to come with her. There was no way she would let me get out of it. I even tried to invent some project that I had to do for school but she wouldn't listen.

I thought I was going to die!

When Mum is in her poet mode she puts on even more dangly earrings than usual. And purple tights! When we were walking to the hall, she kept trying to talk to me in public! So most of the time I just kind of mumbled back to her. I thought anyone who was listening might think I was foreign and nothing to do with her really.

Things started to look a bit more promising at the hall though. There was this Visiting Poet there. He'd come to talk to the Circle and inspire them — so Mum said. I mean this bloke was cool! His name was Qadir Algis and he told everyone that the translation of his name meant Powerful Spear. He was GORGEOUS!

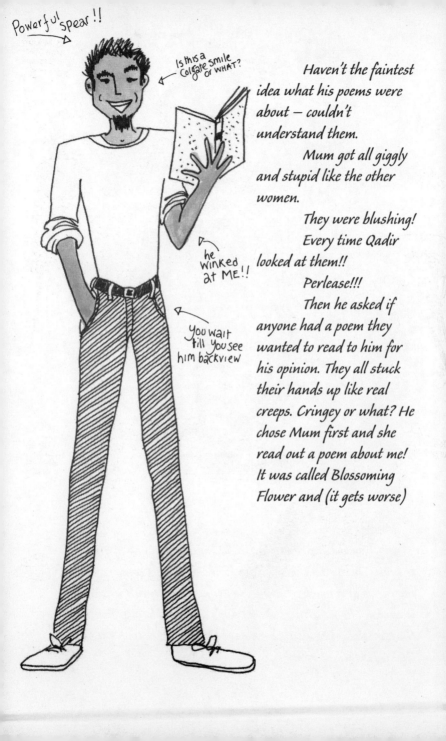

Powerful spear !!

Is this a Colgate smile or WHAT?

he winked at ME!!

you wait till you see him backview

Haven't the faintest idea what his poems were about — couldn't understand them.

Mum got all giggly and stupid like the other women.

They were blushing! Every time Qadir looked at them!!

Perlease!!!

Then he asked if anyone had a poem they wanted to read to him for his opinion. They all stuck their hands up like real creeps. Cringey or what? He chose Mum first and she read out a poem about me! It was called Blossoming Flower and (it gets worse)

it was about when she had me. You know, actually giving birth! How could she do that to me? She told me afterwards that that was why she wanted me to go to the Circle so that I could listen to her poem. I think she actually thought I was going to be pleased that she read a poem about me being born to a whole bunch of nutters and a really fit proper poet. I wanted to die – not be born in a poem in public!

When she'd finished reading it, her earrings were kind of wobbling in rhythm with her shoulders. And all her friends got sucky uppy and started saying things like, 'Oh yes!' and, 'Such emotion!' and, 'Organic!' I thought organic was the stuff my dad sells in his shop? I am sure my real mother

would never do something so terrible to me. No way!

Qadir said that he thought the poem was interesting. He also said that he was pleased to meet the flower from the poem — he winked at me! I think it was a Sign. He knew just how awful it was to have the poem read in public in front of me, didn't he?

Then, after more of them read their ghastly poems, everyone stood around chatting and they each produced a bottle of wine. I kept asking Mum if we could go but she said no. Someone asked if I wanted a drink too, so I said, natch, I'd have a Coke. Mum said no. So I ended up having some warm fizzy water that didn't have any bubbles left. Double yuck.

On the way home, Mum tripped on the pavement — twice. I think she was drunk! Disgusting!

Even worse when we got home, though. Dad was drunk too. He'd been drinking parsley punch with Auntie Melissa and her drippy boyfriend Doug. Nono was there as well but she was having a cup of tea. They were all sitting in the kitchen looking pink and soppy. Except for Nono who was stroking her dog Brian. Giggles hates Brian.

Anyway, things were pretty bad at our house. Everyone was giggling about something and looking really pleased with themselves when Mum and I walked into the living room.

'Amaryllis my petal! Mary! Come in! Have a drink!' Dad bellowed. He always talks really loudly when he's been drinking his nettle beer. The parsley punch seemed to have had the same effect. Anyway, Dad started going on about how we all had something to celebrate.

Mum had this really stupid grin on her face and kept saying, 'Really? Really? How wonderful!'

I hadn't got the faintest idea what was going on but all the old people seemed to. My puke-making brother Hugo was just sitting on the floor with his knees crossed, practising his 'I am an angel' expression.

Dad must have been really gone because he asked
Hugo and me if we wanted some of the parsley punch 'for
toasting tonight's excellent news', even though we still didn't
know what the news was. Hugo, being a toad, said he
preferred water and he'd go and get his own. I said yes —
and regretted it as soon as I tasted the stuff. It was revolting!

25

And on closer inspection it had something floating in it!

Nono asked for another cup of tea and I went to make it for her. This was for two reasons:

☆ if you are nice to Nono she usually gives you money
☆ when I was at the sink I was able to ditch the punch

In the end I made myself a cup of tea as well because it's the only decent drink you can get in our house.

When I gave Nono her tea, she poured some into the saucer and put it down for Brian. Normally Dad would go spare but he was too busy giggling with Auntie Melissa and Doug to say anything. Giggles did though — but only from the other side of the table because he's such a wimp.

Then Dad said, 'Let's have a toast!' And he stuck his glass of parsley punch so high in the air that most of it slopped out and landed on Doug's baldy biscuit head. Doug just laughed and wiped it with Auntie Melissa's cardigan. And Dad said, 'Melissa and Doug! Who are getting married!'

Someone should tell her about those tights that hold your tummy in...

quite like her socks, wonder if she would lend them

hand-painted clogs

Melissa

Is Auntie Melissa mad? She is marrying Doug! He looks half-man, half-dinosaur. He has hair growing out of his ears! OK! magazine will never want to have their wedding in it if she's marrying an ugly pig like him! I mean, OK! won't want photographs like this, will they:

Why does Doug have hair everywhere except where it should be?

weeds

GROOM

BRIDE

matching T-shirts — SICK!

as seen in OK! magazine — oh per-lease

But then, Auntie Melissa is a sort of cardigan person and she'll probably end up with a dress like this knowing her:

Stuffed bird

Knitted top

more weeds

nylon frilly bits

painted-on initials

M and D

red plastic heart

more bows (pink)

After Dad had finished slopping the parsley punch around and Mum had finished saying how lovely everything was. Nono started making big hints about how she needed a lift home and how an hour before ten was worth two hours in the morning. But Auntie Melissa said she had an extra special announcement to make. She said that she wanted me and Hugo to be her bridesmaid and pageboy! DOUBLE DISASTER!

I mean how can I possibly be in the same photograph as Hugo? Or Doug? I just can't!

IS THE REST OF THE WORLD COMPLETELY MAD?

Told Xanthe all about the Circle of Poets and Auntie Melissa on the bus to school this morning. She reckoned that it couldn't be as bad as I said.

her father's a dentist, perhaps she's checking that his teeth are clean

Nora, nice but a bit stinky

school bus

this is the only way to wear a school tie and I always roll my skirt over at the top to make it shorter

Then I reminded her that it was Auntie Melissa and Doug who were getting married — not someone from the telly. 'I see what you mean,' she said, giving me a hug.

Xanthe asked me what I thought my dress was going to be like. I told her it was probably going to be like some kind of cardigan or overall – a bridesmaid version of the sort of thing Melissa normally wears herself. NIGHTMARE!

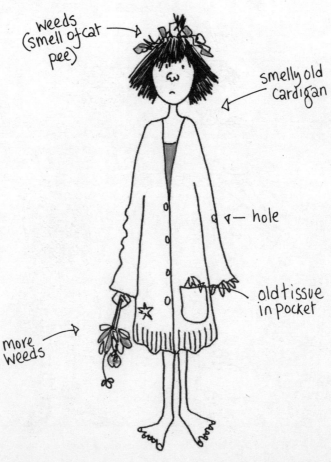

weeds (smell of cat pee)

smelly old cardigan

— hole

old tissue in pocket

more weeds

Will my dress be like this .....?

Or, worse, it could be like a loo-roll cover bought at a church fête.

.... or this?

As we were talking, I spotted that we were being
stared at from the opposite seat. It was Jake's slimy brother
Tarquin. I gave him one of my most sophisticated glares. He
didn't get the hint! Is he that thick? He smiled at us. What did
he think he was up to?

Xanthe got the giggles and smiled back. Then he had
the nerve to speak to us!

'Going to be a bridesmaid, eh?' he said. He had been
listening to everything we'd been saying.

'Have we been speaking loud enough for you, then?' I
said, giving him the evils. Hah! That did it! He went all red
and his spots started to glow. That'll teach him to listen to
private conversations.

Course, if I'd had a mobile, then I'd have been able to

text Xanthe and no one would have been able to listen in, would they? My parents are just so pathetic. They won't even let me have a mobile. It's so unfair!

I mean, I told my mum that absolutely everyone at school has a mobile phone. She said she didn't believe me.

Xanthe's got one. It's really cool and it's got this pink leopardskin cover. I told Mum that if I had a mobile phone, she'd know I was safe because I could text her and tell her I was on my way home from school and stuff. She said she always knew when I was on my way home anyway because school finished at the same time and I always phoned from Nono's if I went there. Anyway she didn't have a mobile phone either and couldn't get texts. She has no clue!

Decided to go and see Nono after school today because:

☆ *she's got a mobile phone with a cow's face on it that goes 'moo' when all her purple-rinsed friends text her, so she'll understand about not having a phone*

☆ *she might be able to persuade Auntie Melissa to change her mind about me being a bridesmaid*

Nono had had a Baking Day! She had platefuls of buns and cakes and other stuff like that. Stuffed my face so that I

yummy buns

Brian's biccies

wouldn't have room for the disgusting mush Mum was bound
to serve up at home. Nono had made some special dog biscuits
for Brian and was feeding him with them like a baby.

Told her about the humiliation of being the only person
in my entire school who hasn't got a mobile phone.

She lent me
these, aren't
they FAB?

Xanthe did
my hair in
break

'No, no,' she said. 'That must be awful, my petal.' She always calls me that because of my name. 'Flowery by name, flowery by nature!' she says. Hmmm. She didn't seem to get the hint about buying me a phone though. Have to try again another day I suppose.

Was eating a gigantic piece of choccy cake when Nono asked if I knew what my bridesmaid's dress was going to be like. Said no but that it was bound to be ghastly. Nono said that under the circumstances everything was being done in a rush.

What did she mean? What circumstances? Thought most people planned weddings for months — years! Posh people get a wedding organizer in and do it properly. It's romantic. I know Auntie Melissa isn't that romantic — and Doug certainly isn't — but why is her wedding being done in a rush?

Nono said that me and Hugo Poogo have got to go for a fitting for our outfits later this week. Mum's going to take us to the long boat. (Auntie Melissa and Doug live on this barge on the canal. Now that could be romantic if the canal didn't have loads of shopping trolleys in it.) She said that Auntie Melissa wants her wedding to be 'at one with nature'. Nono thinks that it means that everything will be made in natural fabrics that can be recycled.

Are we all going to look like hippies? (Might be OK.) Perhaps we'll all look like loo rolls! (Not OK.)

Told Nono that it sounded awful and that I didn't want to be a bridesmaid. She said, 'No, no, dear — I'm sure

38

you'll look lovely. Especially if we choose some sweet little shoes for you to wear.'

She's talking! Wonder if I can persuade her to buy me some wooden wedges?

Left Nono's after taking Brian for a walk. (She gave me £3.50 and I decided to start a mobile phone fund. I mean, if no one else is going to buy me one, I'll have to buy one for myself!)

GOB were emerging from Ben's room when I came up the road to our house. Hugo was sitting on the front wall picking the fleas out of Giggles's coat. Pimply Tarquin was sitting with them (he was probably catching the fleas!) and he had the nerve to smile at me and say hello. Gave him one of my serious glares again because he obviously hasn't got the hint. Disaster though! Just as I was doing my glare, Jake appeared from below ground and landed in front of me.

He is just dreamy! But supposing he thought I was glaring at him! Tried to change it to my most Kylie smile. He didn't say anything. Perhaps he wants to keep it a secret from Ben that he loves me?

JAKE.... I think I'm going to faint. or be sick or both.... ooooh

GOB

I was just about to do my supermodel walk — I've been
practising, in my bedroom — when Mrs Baxter came out of
her house with all her dogs. She's got loads of them.

EEEEEEEK

BONIO

DOGGIE
YUMMIES

Rock
CHICK

She's trying to breed some new dog called a Baxter
Terrier. They were all over the place, as usual. And I got all
tangled up in the leads and tripped over on the pavement.
Tarquin leaped off the wall and made a grab for me. I landed
on the ground with about fifty-five of Mrs Baxter's smelly
dogs licking my face and it was just so not cool. Tarquin pulled
me up. Even worse — Hugo Poogo tried to make out he was

helping me by leaping off the wall too. Giggles bundled straight in and weed on my shoe! Thanks a bunch, Poogo.

Tarquin had the nerve to ask me if I was all right — as if! Gave him the evils again. Jake just grunted and loaded up the GOB van. Think he understood (unlike his stupid brother Tarquin) that less is more. Ben grunted too. I think they were off to some local talent competition to sing their latest number. It's called 'I Don't Want to Get Out of Bed'. Think it's called that because those are the only lyrics and they're sung over and over again. Ben wrote it and Jake sings it. The words are a load of rubbish but Jake makes them sound good.

please don't turn round - PLEASE

Decided that I will never come down the street again without checking for Tarquin and Mrs Baxter.

ALL THIS BRIDESMAID STUFF IS GETTING OUT OF HAND!

Mum was in the kitchen when I got in. She was making nut loaf with onion sauce for supper — puke on a plate! For some reason Mum never seems to have noticed that the only person in our house (apart from her and Dad) who ever eats nut loaf with onion sauce is Hugo. Even Giggles won't touch the stuff I try to shove under the table.

Mum was on her own in the kitchen. Dad wasn't back from the shop and Hugo was being his usual sucky uppy self working on his homework in his room. Get a life, Hugo! Actually, I was quite pleased that I had Mum to myself because it gave me a chance to tell her all the reasons why I shouldn't be a bridesmaid:

45

- I am nearly thirteen
- Hugo is going to be a pageboy (enough said)
- Nono could do with someone to help her walk down the aisle at the wedding. (Tricky one that because Nono doesn't need someone to do this, but she is an OAP and I am sure they are officially meant to have someone helping them regardless)
- a bridesmaid's dress is bound not to suit me
- it's bad news to be a bridesmaid too often (three times a bridesmaid, never a bride, as the saying goes)
- it will be embarrassing
- I don't want to be a bridesmaid
  . . . isn't that enough reasons?

mum is probably thinking about powerful spear— she's NOT LISTENING TO ME

Dad brought this back from the shop 'cos it had a hole in it

wholemeal flour

NUTS

I hate weddings and I hate dogs and I hate nut loaf . . .

Mum was stuffing her nut stuff into a tin while I was talking to her. She was also gazing out of the window at the same time. She hadn't heard a word I had said. So I had to say it all again. My mother is so old and pathetic she just hasn't got any idea about me not being a bridesmaid! She said:

☆ thirteen was the perfect age to be a bridesmaid

☆ being a bridesmaid with Hugo would be sweet

☆ Nono didn't need any help because she was only sixty-three

☆ I'd look lovely in the dress that Auntie Melissa had planned for me (huh!)

☆ I'd never been a bridesmaid before and she couldn't think of many other people who were likely to ask me to be one so I had at least two more attempts to go before I should get worried

☆ it wouldn't be at all embarrassing and I should be flattered to be asked (like she knows!)

☆ I shouldn't just be flattered I should be honoured and keen and eager to help Auntie Melissa

☆ lots of other girls of my age would be pleased to be a bridesmaid and she couldn't understand why I was making such a fuss!

My mother doesn't know anything! And she said that pudding was prunes with semolina. It's just so not fair. Worse, Dad came

47

Frank sometimes poos on Dad's shoulder →

mum put this on. He wears these trousers to WORK! →

▷ Something yukky smelling

Flowerden's Whole Food Wholesome Organic

home with Frank (he's the shop parrot that some old sailor gave to him) and a bag of stuff that was out of date that he couldn't sell any more. Dad said we could have some of it with our supper. Yum, yum . . .

So that was the end of my conversation with Mum about being a bridesmaid. I think that makes it conclusive that I am actually someone else's child and Mum and Dad have just adopted me. I mean, if she really was my mother she would understand the pain, unhappiness and humiliation that I am being put through. I am sure that Xanthe's mum would.

When Ben came home from the talent competition, Mum said, 'Geoffrey, my darling older son,' (she never calls him Ben and I note that she always refers to him as her son — she never calls me her daughter so my point about being adopted is proved) 'how did you get on?' (You see, you can tell she cares more about him than she does about me.)

With Ben, one grunt usually means yes and two grunts mean no. So Mum had to interrogate him some more to get an answer out of him.

'Did you get through to the final, my darling boy?' she crooned.

Ben gave one grunt (or it could have been a burp because he'd just started eating the nut loaf). That means that GOB has got through to the final of a talent competition. Which must mean that either no one else entered or, if they did, they were even worse than GOB. So it must be that no one else entered because even a dead dormouse would be

looking all sweet and innocent

my hair won't lie down after being in bunchies

nasty nut loaf

Ben's place

better than anything that GOB could do.

'Oh Geoffrey, darling son, you are so clever,' Mum
drooled. 'Your little group must play at Auntie Melissa's
wedding.'

Ben grunted again. *Now I've got another reason for
not being at the wedding! I think I am going to die!*

After supper Dad went into the living room to paint
one of his pictures. He asked me to model for him but I said no.
It was enough to be in one of Mum's poems — no way was I
going to be in one of his pictures too.

Dad's version of the Mona Lisa

one of Dad's 'early works'

Wears a smock to paint in

little creep doesn't even mind wearing a wig and a dress — Weirdo

So cue the Poogo: 'Oh dearest father,' he crept. 'May I be of help? Can I please model for you instead of Amaryllis?'

Dad seemed pleased and said yes. Well! He could have said he really needed me, couldn't he? I mean, if he'd begged me, I might have said yes. But he didn't. So Hugo Poogo and Dad went into the living room where Dad was painting yet another picture.

Dad's just entered some competition for someone's summer exhibition of paintings. He's sent in a great big painting of a woman with no clothes on. She looks just like Mum but with blonde hair. When I said that, Mum went all pink and her earrings started to rattle. Nono just choked on her cup of tea and said, 'No, no!' Couldn't agree more.

While the painting-and-sucking-up fest was going on, Mum had one of her clients in for a session so she disappeared up to Ben's old bedroom. Nowadays she calls it her Therapy Suite. As if! Ben just disappeared into the cellar as per usual. So I was on my own. I was OK with that.

Unlike absolutely everyone else at school I not only don't have a) a television in my room and b) my own shower room, but I also don't have c) a phone in my room. In fact the only phone in our house is in the hallway. So it is almost impossible to have a private conversation with anyone. Another reason for needing a mobile! But, with Ben in the cellar, Dad in the living room with Hugo and Mum upstairs with a client, the coast was clear.

I rang Xanthe to tell her about the disaster in front of Jake when I got home from Nono's. The only problem was Frank.

He sat on the banister swearing.
        Wish I could work out what I did to deserve all this!

MOBILE PHONE FUND TOTAL: £3.56 (money left over from last wodge of money Nono gave me for walking Brian).

TOTAL WORLD
HUMILIATION!

*Have decided that I would rather be Frank than a bridesmaid.
Excrutiating embarrassment and total world humiliation
today...*

*Went with Mum and Hugo to Auntie Melissa's long
boat (it's called The Doug 'n' Mel ... Puke!). We were supposed
to go to see her for a fitting for our wedding outfits. It wasn't
so much a fitting as a try-this-on-it's-just-perfect-for-you-
and-I-am-sure-that-you-can-squeeze-into-it sort of thing.*

*Am so horrified by what I saw I am seriously
considering running away. That would teach my mum to be so
I'm-your-mother-and-I-know-what's-best-for-you-ish. And
it will teach Auntie Melissa too.*

*Get this! The whole wedding is going to be themed and
Auntie Melissa has chosen the theme of The Nature of the*

World. I ask you! What does that mean? It means Auntie Melissa is nuts — that's what it means. Can you believe it? Hugo is going to represent the moon and I have got to represent the sun. Auntie Melissa has got so fat that she's probably going to represent the entire world and all the planets in the universe. Doug is so wet he's probably all the seas and oceans . . .

Was given this completely stupid baby dress with all these gross frills and daggy bits on it. Worse, it was bright orange! To match the sun. I look like a bottle of that disgusting orange squash that they serve up in school for parties.

A HEAD-DRESS AAAARRGH!!!

fake sunflowers, I'd rather have real stinky ones

This bib bit is strapped over a whole ORANGE dress with a frilly skirt

this is all ORANGE NET

Told Auntie Melissa that there was no way I was going to wear it but Mum said I had to and would I just look at myself in the mirror to see how lovely I looked? Is my mother blind? Told them both I looked like a pizza someone had sicked up on the pavement but Mum just got cross with me and Auntie Melissa said she had a twinge and needed to sit down. Can't see why anything I said would make her feel ill.

moon thing ties up under his chin

look at him — he LIKES his moon outfit

this bit buttons on to his starry suit

full moon and cloud

frilly bits, meant to be more clouds

Of course Hugo Poogo got completely toad-like and told them both how fantastic he thought his moon costume looked and, 'Please could I wear it on the way home?' Cringe!

After that, Mum just kept giving me the evils and told Auntie Melissa that she needed to get her rest and put her feet up. Auntie Melissa was wearing this cutesy T-shirt with a bear on the front. It had a slogan across her boobs that said 'Seed Pod'. Mum kept saying she was doing too much. Doing too much what? She's only getting married. And making me dress up like a Jaffa Cake without the chocolate on the outside.

When we were leaving, Mum hissed at me and said that I had to apologize to Auntie Melissa for being so rude and ungrateful. I was only telling the truth! Dad is always saying that it's best to tell the truth rather than tell a lie. But when I *do, see what good it does me?*

*Told Mum I would only apologize if she made
cauliflower cheese for supper. She said it was a deal so I put on
my cheesiest grin and said sorry. Auntie Melissa then came
out with all this rot about me being her favourite niece and
how much it meant to her that I was a bridesmaid.*

I am the only niece she's got, aren't I? Pathetic.

Auntie Melissa is keeping her dress a secret until the

horrible
coffee

She really is
<u>very</u> fat

*Big Day as Mum keeps on calling it. A secret from who?
Martians? What worries me is, if my dress looks so awful,
what's hers going to be like?*

one of mum's
clients

Mum had a client waiting on the doorstep when we got home.
Another one of her women with a moustache. Think I want to
be a therapist when I'm older. I'm sure I could solve their
problems better than Mum can. Just tell them, shave and all
your worries will be over. Sorted.

CHEMICAL
FREE
ZONE

THE
WONDER
WORMERY

this is my bra
I'm just about
to grow into it

So Mum whizzed off to her Therapy Room and Hugo disappeared into the garden to look for more worms to add to his wormery, which he's making for some conservation project at school. Dad was still at the shop, probably bagging up more dust to sell. So there was no one to give me any scoff and nothing, as per usual, in the fridge. Then I remembered that Nono had matching air-tight boxes stuffed with delicious nosh. So I left a note on the kitchen table and legged it to her house.

When I got there, Nono was watching a quiz on her surround sound telly. She let me in with her video entry phone — it's her latest gadget. Nono likes gadgets: she's got these really cool electric curtains that open and close at the touch of one of her remote control units. Once she went to answer her phone and accidentally closed the curtains and switched off the telly at the same time. But when I got to Nono's today, she

Why is Nono knitting booties?

this is a massage chair, it sort of trembles when you switch it on some of Nono's gadgets

mooing mobile phone

was sitting on her massage chair (it kind of wobbles, to shake up your muscles) with Brian at her feet. She was knitting. I could see some little boot things on the knitting needles.

Suddenly, it all sank into place! The reason why:

☆ Auntie Melissa is so fat
    and
☆ Auntie Melissa is marrying Doug
    and
☆ I have got to look like part (the rotten part) of a fruit salad
    and
☆ Nono says everything is having to be done in a rush
    and
☆ Auntie Melissa had to rest and put her feet up its

because . . .

SHE IS HAVING A BABY!

The bootees that Nono was making were for her baby. This means that Auntie Melissa and Doug must have actually done it. Gross! This also means that Auntie Melissa's baby will look like a combination of Auntie Melissa and Doug! Poor kid.

Nono gave me a plateful of gorgeousness to eat and in between mouthfuls I told her about the bridesmaid's dress. Nono says that Auntie Melissa doesn't want any of us to wear shoes for

It's not fat
it's a BA

Peach

the wedding! She says that Auntie Melissa thinks that bare feet will make us feel the power of nature through our feet. Nono also says that we will all tread in dog poo and get other people's verrucas so she handed me a wodge of money and told me to go out and buy myself some shoes to wear with the dress.

Nice one, Nono! Will go with Xanthe to buy something cool on Saturday.

Just thought, as I am not nearly as weird looking as any of my family, that must be another thing that proves I really belong to someone else. Probably my real father is a rock star and my mother is someone who fell madly in love with

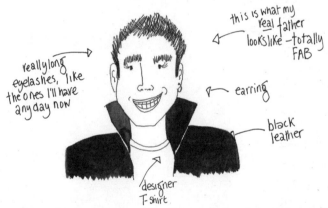

really long eyelashes, like the ones I'll have any day now

this is what my real father looks like – totally FAB

earring

black leather

designer T-shirt

him. When I find out who my rock star dad is, he will be really pleased to discover me and offer to take me away from here to live in his house in California.

MOBILE PHONE FUND: £5.56 (topped up with £2 from shoe fund – Nono won't mind!)

SHOES – SIMPLY THE BEST THINGS IN THE WORLD

Went round to Xanthe's this morning to check out her mum's magazines. I love going to Xanthe's house because it is just so brilliant. For a start, nothing in Xanthe's house has had a former life as something belonging to the council (unlike my house). Everything in it is just, well, perfect. The paintings on the walls do not look like blonde naked versions of Xanthe's mum. And the carpets do not look as if they have got something living in them. Even Xanthe's cat, Pandora, is elegant. She doesn't leave her fur in the butter like Giggles.

Anyway, magazines. Xanthe's got some really great ones – Vogue, OK!, Hello! That sort of stuff. My mum never buys magazines because she says they are the price of a good book but without the educational value. What does she mean? Vogue's got loads of ideas for gorgeous dresses so surely that makes it good value. And OK! and Hello! are full of photos of really fit people. Unlike the only magazines we have in our house, which are bought by Dad and are called things like Composting Today and Wholefooders', United. Yum, yum! Not.

Xanthe's mum, Tasmin, was there and gave us this huge pile of wedding magazines she had. Tasmin is such a fab name. It's not a mum's name at all. Anyway, because Xanthe's mum makes jewellery, she'd got all these magazines because they'd had bits in them about the stuff she makes. Xanthe's mum is completely cool and wears these really OK clothes. Unlike my mum, Xanthe's mum would not be seen dead in a pair of purple tights.

All the bridesmaids in the magazines had these

gorgeous dresses — they looked like proper bridesmaids, not like something from a bad circus. And they all had decent shoes on. Told Xanthe about being 'at one' with nature and she said it made her feel a bit sick. Supposing, she said, someone had spat on the pavement! Eugh! We went straight out to buy shoes as soon as she said that.

Fell completely in love with a pair of trainers that we spotted. Even nicer than wooden wedges. They were pretty delicious as they were but Xanthe reckoned if we glued some beads from her mum's jewellery on them, they would look the

the most totally FAB trainers

Xanthe is going to look after them for me

business. Am sure that Xanthe is right. Decided to keep them at Xanthe's house so that they were safe from:

☠ my mum finding them

☠ Giggles doing a wee on them

☠ Hugo thinking they are something he can grow something in

We went back to Xanthe's house for lunch because Xanthe's dad had promised to make us something Indian. Got off the

a total babe like me does **not** want to be seen with a twit like him

quite nice jersey, he probably pinched it from Jake

bus at the end of Xanthe's road and were just walking to her house when we spotted that twit Tarquin again! He was sitting on the wall opposite Xanthe's house.

He is stalking me. On the bus, then at my house and now he's at Xanthe's.

I gave the creep a bit of verbal. 'Haven't you got a home?'

He, being a smarty pants, said, 'This is my home! I live here!'

As if! Xanthe called me in for lunch then. So I walked, completely cool, into her house. That showed him! Boys! They think they are so sorted! Yeah, right.

We were hanging out in Xanthe's bedroom after lunch so that we could listen to records and stuff. Xanthe has got:

☆ her own telly
☆ her own CD player
☆ her own computer
☆ her own phone
☆ her own DVD player

It is just so not fair! Everyone else in my school has got them too. Anyway, Xanthe had this really cool DVD that we were watching and it had this great music on it. So we started dancing to it in front of the mirror. And that was when I saw Tarquin! He was staring at me from the upstairs window of the house opposite. Unbelievable. I can't dance in my bedroom because Hugo says I sound like a herd of elephants. Like, what would he know? But now I can't dance in Xanthe's bedroom

either because Tarquin stares through the window.

What was he doing there? Xanthe said that she thought maybe he did live there because, come to think of it, maybe she had seen him around before. But Xanthe also said that she just so didn't need to look at boys at the moment that she hadn't really paid any attention to him. Which was a bit of a weird thing really. I mean, Xanthe's usually really into boys and I said so. But Xanthe just looked a bit mizzy and said she had other things to think about at the moment.

'Like what?' I asked but she said she didn't really want to talk about it. I felt bad. I mean, Xanthe's my best friend and I'd been rabbiting on about all my stuff and hadn't asked her how she was. And now Xanthe didn't want to talk. Gave her a hug, though, and she smiled. But I still don't know why she was fed up.

In the end I had to go home because it was getting late. Tasmin gave me a fabby bracelet before I left. Xanthe's dad gave me some of the stuff he'd cooked to take home with me. He said that it was because he'd made extra and he thought my parents might like it. I expect the reason he said that is because he knows the kind of sawdust we have to eat at home and he was feeling sorry for me. Looked up at the house opposite when I crossed the road outside Xanthe's. Tarquin was standing at the window again. He waved at me!

Actually, he looked quite cute. But I didn't wave back. I was cool.

MOBILE PHONE FUND: £5.61 (found 5p on the pavement when walking home).

THE WEDDING THAT WON'T BE
IN ANY MAGAZINES
AT ALL

The morning of the wedding was kind of weird. Went down for breakfast in my normal clothes and hoped that Mum would let me slip off to the wedding in them. Course she wouldn't — Rats! Hugo Poogo was so excited and squirmy nice about wearing his moon stuff that he practically wanted to eat his breakfast in it. Little squirt!

    Mum got changed first and came down looking a bit like a sofabed. She had on this long sort of flowery thing — I think it was meant to be a dress. And she had this floppy hat on. Her earrings were all dingly dangly too. She was in such a good mood that she was humming and saying, 'Isn't it a wonderful day?' All the time. That's why I thought I might get

I don't know how long she's had this DRESS

Fringey bag is actually quite trendy but Mum doesn't know that

It's got lacey bits round the bottom

Mum's outfit

away with not wearing my Sunny Delight. Fat chance!

Mum had to bellow down into the cellar to get Ben out of his pit. He came up (eventually) grunting and wearing the same T-shirt I think he has been wearing for the past year. Mum didn't tell him to change. It's just so NOT FAIR!

Dad was lurking about in something very similar to what he wears every day. Sandals without socks (I mean, YUCK!), rather baggy cord trousers with faded bits, a sort of hairy shirt and one of those jumper things that Nono is always knitting for him. The only thing that was different

little bit of net with a wobbly flower

you just sort of know that she's got sweeties in here

she's not going to risk squishing into something in the grass

Nono's Wedding Outfit

about him was that he'd put a daisy in his buttonhole.

Nono arrived just after breakfast. She looked cool. In fact, she looked like she was going to a wedding. And she had these really gorgeous shoes on with pointy toes and kitten heels.

'Amaryllis,' she said, 'I will not go barefoot anywhere in a public place!' Then she whispered, 'Have you got your new shoes?' You bet I had!

Nono had been very busy knitting. Although she usually only knits jumper things for Dad, she's really good at

Nono had to tie the hat on under his ears!

knitting – she can knit anything. For the wedding she'd been busy knitting for Giggles and Brian. She'd knitted them top hats and jackets with bow ties. Brian and Giggles were going to be the only two guests – apart from Nono, of course – who looked good enough to be in a magazine photograph. Except I don't think Giggles was very happy about it. Of course, he's never happy about anything.

Nono was in the middle of getting the dogs dressed (she had to tie a hanky around Giggles's muzzle to stop him from snarling so much) when the postman came. Usually Dad just groans when the post arrives and hides the envelopes in the breadbin. But when the post arrived that day, he went all mental. He ripped open an envelope, read the letter and then ran up and down the hallway screaming. He showed the letter to Mum and she ran up and down the hallway screaming too. Nono asked if they were feeling OK and they said, 'Read this letter.' She did. Nono didn't let out a scream but she did kind of gasp and say, 'Oh my goodness.'

Hugo Poogo put on his best goody gumdrops voice and said, 'Daddy dearest what is the good news?'

And then Dad told us. He told us that he had had one of his paintings accepted for some exhibition in London over

74

the summer.

Big deal, eh? I mean, from the way he and Mum were carrying on, you'd have thought that he was actually going to appear on the telly or something important like that. Instead, he's going to hang up a picture of one of those blonde, Mum lookalikes in some dusty old gallery. Like, so?

When he'd finished jumping up and down, something even weirder happened. Dad went upstairs to change. He came down wearing a beret and carrying some paintbrushes. Groan. My dad now thinks he is a proper Artist . . .

look what he's got on his head! He thinks he looks 'arty'

he says that now he's a 'Proper Artist' he must take his paint brushes everywhere

Hawaiian shirt

I bet he's put the paint splodges on specially

bell bottoms!!

Dad didn't do anything to the car to make it look remotely cool for the wedding. He didn't even decorate it with ribbons. He couldn't even drive it because he was so excited. So

we all bundled into it and Nono drove us, with *Flowerdew and Sons and Daughter* written along the side of us. How cool was that? Not.

The wedding was taking place on the common next to the bandstand. Some people were already there when we arrived. Actually it was quite difficult to work out which one was Doug at first because all his friends and family look just like him. Weird. Yuck — who wants more than one Doug?? Must be a bit confusing for Auntie Melissa. Imagine you think you are kissing Doug and you're actually smooching with his Uncle Billy — aaaggh!!!

But then I spotted Auntie Melissa and she was holding Doug's hand — so that was a bit of a clue. At least I assumed it was Doug because she kept looking all gooey-eyed at him.

I have never seen a wedding dress like Auntie Melissa's before. It was gross. She must have made it herself. You couldn't possibly buy something like it in a shop.

The woman who was going to do the wedding arrived and the ceremony began. I was expecting someone dressed up in some kind of cape or something. Actually she was quite normal, in a dinner-lady kind of way.

Hugo stood grinning like a twit as the dinner lady said all this stuff about love and commitment.

Auntie Melissa and Doug had these cheesy grins.

Dad spent the whole time holding up his hands and making a square shape with them that he looked through — just like he does when he is painting someone.

Worse! I think my mum was crying. She certainly kept blowing her nose. And her eyes were sparkly.

Nono didn't cry, but she did keep shaking her head and clicking her tongue.

After the nylon wedding lady had finished, Auntie Melissa and Doug asked everyone to hold hands and form circles round the trees. I certainly wasn't going to hold hands and hug a tree with anyone — even if he wasn't actually Doug and just looked like him. Nono just said, 'No, no!' and went to sit down near the bandstand. She had to move pretty quickly, though, when GOB started up.

nylon hair

nylon suit

Giggles tried to bite her and laddered her tights

something sticky

she's allowed to wear shoes

Jake tuning up

he's so cool he can wear a roll neck on a hot day and still stay fridge fresh

BOG

GOB

Ben practising a 'roll' or a 'bun' or something

what's he doing? SPYING

XANTHE SAVES ME FROM THE PIT OF DEATH!

Managed to slink off in Nono's shadow and sit down next to
her. But it was just awful because suddenly I heard all this
yelling and giggling. It was some boys from school. I think
they'd been playing football and they were falling over
themselves laughing at all those Dougs hugging trees. If I
hadn't been part of it, I would have joined them. But, instead,
I had to try to disguise myself as a tree — which is a bit
difficult when you've got a bright orange dress on.

I don't think they saw me though because it was at
exactly that moment that Xanthe appeared from behind the
loos! She is a star. And she seemed a bit happier than the
other day. Xanthe brought what she called the Rescue Kit
with her:

☆ my fabby new trainers
☆ make up
☆ a pair of scissors
☆ my cycling shorts.

After a bit of snipping with the scissors my bridesmaid's dress began to look way better. Xanthe is just brill at that sort of thing. She managed to give my dress a kind of tutu effect.

loads of really fab stuff AND MY SHOES

Boot Bag

gorgeous skirt—sparkly bits AND fringey bits

With that, my trainers, my cycle shorts and the application of a little subtle make up, I looked much more like a normal bridesmaid. Xanthe said there was absolutely nothing she could do to make my headdress look even remotely respectable so I just chucked that in the bin.

When we came out of the loo, Nono was sticking some ear plugs in. GOB had really got going. They were doing a cover version of 'Here Comes the Bride'. Jake looked so cool!

I think he winked at me when he saw me in my tutu thingy.
Xanthe said she thought he was just wincing because there

here he is
AGAIN!
Why is she
outside
the
'Ladies' loo?

my WONDERFUL
shoes!!
(yes, I did wash my feet
before I put them on)

was a problem with the amplifier but I know she wasn't right.
We were just talking about it when Tarquin came round the
side of the bogs.

'Nice dress,' he said. What exactly did that mean? I

mean, what was he doing round by the side of the loo anyway? Why is Tarquin everywhere I go these days? Didn't know what to say to him so I dragged Xanthe off to find Nono. Tarquin stared at me all the way over to where Nono was. So I stared back when we sat down. Hah!

I always thought weddings had nice food that was served by waiters. But not Auntie Melissa's and Doug's wedding. We had to sit down on rugs on the grass and have a picnic. (I was glad I had my shoes on because Nono kept saying that she thought there was Something Rather Nasty Down There.)

Mum had made all sorts of brown food and handed

great bowlfuls of it to everyone. She was doing cheesy grins a lot and flirting with all the Dougs. Someone of her age!

Nono hadn't made brown food. She'd made muffins and cup cakes and nice things, so Xanthe and I stuffed ourselves with her nosh. Delish! There wasn't much good stuff to drink though. Dad and Doug had spent the last few weeks making nettle beer and dandelion fizz on Doug 'n' Mel. I think they thought it was smart to serve that at a wedding. But then what do they know? Movie stars never have nettle beer and dandelion fizz at their weddings, do they?

Nono had brought along some drink she'd made called

Rocket. Xanthe and I tried it — eeugh! It was completely foul! But the disgusting taste didn't seem to stop any of the grown-ups from drinking it. In fact when GOB took a break from playing, they seemed to drink rather a lot of it. Especially Jake. Was sure that he winked at me again but Xanthe said that he was just squinting because he had the sun in his eyes and that actually it was Tarquin who was winking at me. Is she mad?

Tarquin was leaning against the bandstand sorting out the speakers or whatever it is he does as the roadie for GOB. When he saw Xanthe and I didn't have anything to drink, he came over and offered us some of his water.

After we'd drunk it and he'd gone back to being a roadie, I asked Xanthe if she knew what Tarquin's problem was. She said she didn't think he had one and that he was just being nice and friendly. Hmm. Then Xanthe said she thought that Auntie Melissa and Doug looked really happy.

'Happy! After the most embarrassing wedding in the world?' I said.

Xanthe got a bit huffy with me after that. She said that smart, expensive weddings didn't make people love each other. It wasn't what things looked like but how things were that really mattered. Then she went into a kind of sulk.

I didn't have much of a clue what she was on about so I ate one of Nono's chocolate brownies with extra chocolate chips. Xanthe looked terrible. I couldn't even persuade her to eat a brownie either. So I asked her what was wrong. And she said that I didn't know how lucky I was.

'Me?' I said. 'Lucky? To live with this lot?'

But Xanthe looked at me with these weird eyes and told me how lucky I was because my mum and dad really loved me and they really loved each other too. And Hugo and Ben. I couldn't understand what she meant and I told her that she was the lucky one because her mum and dad were just so cool and had a really fab house. Xanthe just sat there and cried. Awful.

MOBILE PHONE FUND: £5.61 (found 5p on the common and discovered the 5p I found the other day was actually a Euro. Huh!)

glaring at Brian

watching Giggles

...dwich to ...less ...tummy

even Giggles won't eat nut loaf

trying a lentil and garlic sandwich

FAMILIES ARE JUST TOO EMBARRASSING FOR WORDS

Eventually I persuaded Xanthe to have one of Nono's blueberry muffins and she seemed to cheer up a bit. I still couldn't understand why she was quite so upset, though.

After the picnic, people started to get in the mood for dancing (sad but true) and the music got louder so it was difficult to chat with her. Unfortunately, my mum and dad got up to dance . . . I mean, all I can say is WHY???? There was my mum with her earrings and all her wobbly bits and there was my dad with his paintbrushes. What did I ever do to deserve this public humiliation? Mind you, all the Doug-alikes were so jolly after the nettle beer and dandelion fizz that they were doing some dance too — one they called the Twist. Perlease! Xanthe wanted to dance though and GOB didn't sound too bad — they were playing their new song 'I Found It

In The Fridge'. It was cool — geddit? Anyway, if you were dancing, it meant that you didn't have to watch everyone else dancing and embarrassing themselves.

Nono was just about the only person who wasn't dancing. She was too busy with her camcorder. Auntie Melissa and Doug had said that they didn't want a video of the wedding because they just wanted 'to remember the magic in the air', but Nono said, 'No, no, I insist — a video will be the only way for you to remember absolutely everything that happens on the day.' Actually, I think Nono wanted to have it all on film because she knew that none of her friends would believe her when she told them how weird the whole thing had been.

After a quick bop, me and Xanthe took a breather. She'd definitely cheered up. But that's when everything got really bad because some man arrived with a camera saying he was a photographer from the local paper. He wanted to take photographs of all of us because he said it was such a special wedding. I only wish he had been kidding. I'm just glad Xanthe had managed to rescue my dress before he arrived!

Auntie Melissa and Doug got all stupid cupid when the photographer was there and they asked everyone to hold hands again to make another Circle of Love for him. They stood in the middle of the circle sucking each others faces. Yuck! Xanthe and I tried to hide behind one of the Doug-alikes. Well how can we go to school on Monday knowing that everyone is going to see us Circling Love next to the bandstand on the common?

Then Dad got all chatty with the photographer and offered him some of his nettle beer. He was waving his paintbrushes around

— huge eyebrows and No hair

— doesn't smile – ever

while he talked and the photographer kept writing things in his notebook. As if my dad has ever said anything interesting enough for anyone else to write down!

GOB took a break again after that and two Doug-alikes got up on the bandstand to sing some soppy songs and play guitars. Worse, when they finished, Mum (I think she was drunk) got completely carried away and pushed Hugo up on the bandstand to sing. He did 'Walking in the Air' like he did at the school Christmas concert. He was just as awful then, too, doing his angel impression.

There are a number of reasons why I hate Hugo:

- he is my brother and that's reason enough on its own
- everyone thinks he is so cute
- Hugo thinks he is so cute
- he sings solo at things like weddings and actually likes it
- he is an all-round creep
- he likes homework.

I hope a really big blue bottle flies right down his throat

It was simply too embarrassing to listen to Hugo. I looked round and noticed that Jake was standing with Ben and the others drinking some more nettle beer. So I grabbed Xanthe's hand and started to drag her over there. I thought this might be my chance actually to get to speak to Jake before he started to sing again.

But we hadn't even got there when there was this terrible crash. Jake had fallen over into all the recycled beer

he NEEDS me.....

bottles! The noise was horrific — I thought Jake might have cut
himself. So I ran over there, JUST IN TIME FOR JAKE TO LIFT
HIS HEAD UP AND RAINBOW CAKE ALL OVER MY
GORGEOUS NEW TRAINERS.

I think I hate Jake.

HOW CAN A GIRL LOOK COOL WITH PUKE ON HER SHOES?

So there I am, standing in my Jaffa Cake tutu with Jake's puke all over my feet. Jake didn't even say sorry. He just lay there moaning and then went dead quiet. Ben did a lot of grunting (not even at me) and then he and the others pushed off into the back of their van and left it to Tarquin to bundle him in. Then they drove off!

I'm like, shoes – puke! Puke – shoes! My shoes are covered in puke!

And they just drove off!

They didn't even wait for Tarquin.

Nono came over and said, 'Oh no, no!' and produced a pair of rubber gloves from her handbag. She told me to sit in the back of the car and use them to take the

I expect
Nono's got
loo paper in here
as well, just in
case

GOB's van

they tried to paint over the name

JUICY CHOP BUTCHER

GOB

gross pig— total trainer trasher, I HATE him.

shoes off. I love Nono. She is the only person I know who travels with rubber gloves for emergencies. And I hate Jake for puking on my new shoes. Mum and Dad were too busy singing songs, with the Doug-alikes playing their guitars, even to notice my distress.

Xanthe and I were just trying to find somewhere to dump the rainbowed trainers when Tarquin appeared and said, 'Here! Put them in this.' He had this plastic bag and he took the shoes off in it to put them in the bin. Then he came back and said, 'Sorry about my brother, Amaryllis.' He knew my name!

I was just about to say, 'That's OK,' when I realized it wasn't at all OK. Instead I said, 'They were new!' and Tarquin said he was really sorry again. So I said, 'Well, your brother wasn't!'

And he said, 'I know, he was well out of order.'

I didn't really know what to say after that. But, fortunately, I didn't have to think of anything smart because that was when Dad made some cringey announcement about Auntie Melissa and Doug going off on their honeymoon to start their new life together and everyone started cheering and yelling. Yawn yawn!

Auntie Melissa and Doug don't have a car. As if!

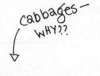

Instead, they've got a bike with a trailer (natch!). A Doug-alike and Hugo were looking very pleased with themselves because they'd decorated the bike with bits of old string and bean tins from Dad's shop. They'd put a sign on the back of the bike that said 'U 2 R 1 (and soon 3!)'. I suppose the Doug-alikes thought that was funny. Auntie Melissa and Doug seemed to. They are so sad.

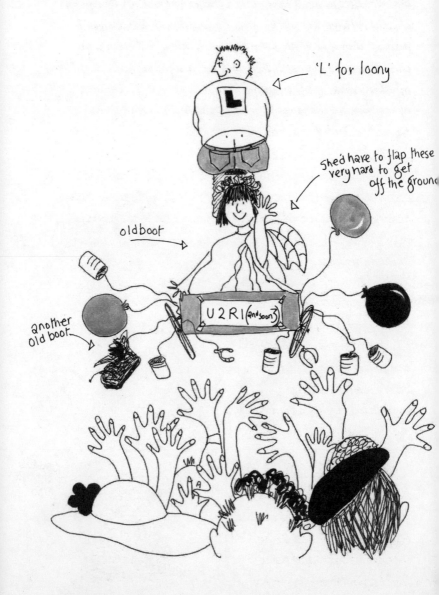

As Auntie Melissa was helped ino the trailer (and she needed rather a lot of help), the Doug-alikes handed round bags of brown rice. We were meant to throw brown rice at them instead of confetti! Perlease! Can't my family do anything done at a normal wedding?

So there I was, without any shoes and expected to trample across the Something-Rather-Nasty-Is-Down-There bit of grass to throw rice at Auntie Melissa and her new husband. That was when I realized that Nono was almost certainly right about the grass (even though none of the Doug-alikes or my mum and dad seemed to care) and that Doug was now my uncle. There is absolutely no way that I am going to call him Uncle Doug!

Decided to throw my rice from exactly where I was standing with Xanthe rather than slip in something slimy (I'd had enough of slimy stuff for one day).

Mum was definitely crying this time. In fact, she didn't seem to care if anyone was looking. Dad put his arm round her. In public!

this is the real one, not the stupid one on Hugo's head

By now, Giggles was howling at the moon (shame he didn't howl like that at Hugo Poogo too) and Brian was curled up round Nono's feet, keeping them warm.

sounds better than Hugo

Xanthe can phone her mum any time because she's got a MOBILE PHONE

BOOTY BAG

Xanthe rang her mum and dad and asked if they could come and get her so that she could go home.

Nono gave us some chewing gum and said, 'Don't let your father see it.'

Hugo said he didn't want any, 'Thank you'. Creep! Then he went off to look for mini beasts on the common. I reckon he'd frighten the mini beasts off! Come to think of it, I reckon Hugo IS a mini beast.

It was only Xanthe's mum who came to get her that night. She didn't stay and chat like she usually did. She didn't look cool and trendy like she usually did either. In fact she was wearing a tracksuit and she didn't have any make up on. Xanthe looked a bit embarrassed. I mean, I'm used to being embarrassed by my parents but I've never seen Xanthe look like that before. She looked sad when she waved goodbye and left.

Now it was just really our lot left at the bandstand and Nono kept making hints about wanting to get back in time to watch something on the telly. So we got the picnic stuff together, recovered our own mini beast from his nature hunt (I noticed he was putting things in his pockets — DISGUSTING!) and I realized that I had no choice but to walk in my bare feet.

104

Except that I didn't! Tarquin appeared again (don't know where he'd been since he took my pukey trainers though) and said, 'Here, I'll help', and he picked me up and carried me to the car!

Weirdly, it wasn't like, hello I can walk you know. In fact, it was cool. And I didn't have to tread in anything.

Tarquin put me down right by the car and held the door open for me while I got in. He said, 'See you soon, Amaryllis. Thought you were really cool today.' Then he went.

I'm, like, totally gobsmacked! Of course, if I had a phone, I could have rung Xanthe and told her all about it. Only

I haven't, have I? Thanks to my parents . . .

    Nono had to drive Dad's car home (again) on account of the fact that she was the only one who hadn't been drinking nettle beer who could drive. Grown-ups . . . more like groan-ups!

STOP THE WORLD. I WANT TO GET OFF!

Sunday. Boring old Sunday. Nothing going on in our house because:

ꙮ Ben is in a coma down in the cellar after drinking all that nettle beer at the wedding

ꙮ Dad is in a coma upstairs after drinking all that nettle beer at the wedding

ꙮ Mum is in a semi-coma upstairs after getting

in a coma (as usual) →

snoring and dribbling a bit

NIRVANA

so emotional at the wedding

🔞 *Hugo is in the garden doing Something Unpleasant with Something Unpleasant*

🔞 *Giggles is in a coma in the kitchen making the most DISGUSTING smells after eating too much at the wedding.*

I don't want to look greedy, but....

mum letting the moths out of her purse!

glitter glue down seams

edges fray by me

might paint flowers on the old things, like Melissa's sho

Mum stumbled downstairs. She must have been hung over because she gave me some money to buy sweets! So I decided to go to the corner shop to see if I had enough money to get a magazine as well. After all, my parents weren't in a fit state to notice.

Mr Kumar at the corner shop was dead excited when I went in there. 'Have you seen this?' he kept saying, pointing to the local paper, Sunday Sensation Local. I mean, how could I have seen it if I had only just gone into his shop? 'Look,' Mr Kumar said. 'Your family is famous!'

It was at exactly that moment that I decided I wanted to disappear from the planet. There, on the front of the local paper, was a picture of my dad in his artist's beret. Complete with cheesy grin and a Smug Factor of about 25. The headline said something about my dad being a painter. Underneath there was a load of stuff about my dad's painting being chosen for something called the Summer Exhibition at some place in London called the Royal Academy of Art. Honestly, you'd have thought my dad's picture had been chosen to be in something famous the way the article went on.

So stuff the idea about buying a decent magazine. Instead I spent the money buying sweets and as many copies of the local paper as I could afford. I figured that if I bought most of Mr Kumar's stock then no one else in the area would be able to buy one and then maybe we could keep my embarrassing dad a secret.

When I got home I stuffed most of the papers on the compost heap and then took one into the kitchen to read. Double horror! When I got to the end of the article it said, 'Artist's Family in Double Celebration Party — See Page 4'. Sure enough, on page

four was the most humiliating selection of photographs of my family I think I have ever seen. They'd all been taken by that photographer bloke at Auntie Melissa's wedding. There was:

a photograph of Nono with Giggles and Brian — the only passable photograph

a photograph of Mum and Dad doing the twist – looking more like Dum and Mad

a crowd scene of the Doug-alikes

a picture of Jake out cold on the grass — just before they carted him off

a perfectly disgusting photograph of Hugo

There was also a photograph of me trying to hide behind the loos. Only it was so obviously me.

How can I possibly go to school tomorrow? The whole world will know that I come from a family of lunatics!

I went round to Xanthe's to show her the ghastly news. She didn't want me to come into the house because she said her parents were having a row!!!! Weird! So we went and sat on the common for a bit. We kept away from the bandstand area in case:

   💡 someone in my family or one of the Doug-alikes had done something awful with lasting damage the day before

   💡 anyone who had read the local paper happened to be there and recognized me.

Fortunately we were left on our own and I showed Xanthe the damage. She said it wasn't so bad and that there were plenty of other much worse things happening in the world. Huh!

'Nothing even half as bad as Auntie Melissa's wedding has ever happened in your family I bet!' I said. But she just looked at me.

Told Xanthe about Tarquin carrying me back to the car. She looked dead surprised and I said, 'Awful, isn't it?'

She said no it wasn't and that she thought it was actually romantic and I should be totally grateful that something so lovely had happened and how she wished she was me last night being someone special at the wedding and having a hunk like Tarquin interested in me.

116

What is she on about? What does she mean? Is Tarquin a hunk? He's nothing like his brother Jake, but then I hate his brother Jake now. And how does she know that Tarquin is interested in me?

Then Xanthe said that she had to get home because it was nearly lunch time. She looked miserable. Don't think I've ever seen Xanthe so mizz.

So I said, 'What's wrong, Xanthe?' I asked her if something had happened and said, 'Cheer up — nothing as dreadful as Doug and Auntie Melissa having a mini-Doug could ever be your problem.'

But Xanthe said it was! She said a fat lot I knew about things — that her mum and dad seemed to row instead of speaking these days and that sometimes her dad didn't even come home any more because he said all Tasmin ever did was shout at him and ask him if he had a girlfriend! Talk about gobsmacked.

Poor old Xanthe.

It was hard to believe. After all, her mum and dad are like Mr and Mrs Perfect. They are gorgeous to look at and have great clothes and a brilliant house. But now Xanthe was saying that it was desperate at home and my house was better because at least my mum and dad loved all of us. I'd never thought about it really.

Told Xanthe that if I had a mobile phone, I would call her and text her all evening to make her feel better. Only I haven't got a mobile so I could only give her a hug instead. She looked really sad when she went.

When I got home, everyone was going bananas again. Turned out that while I was out, Dad had had a call from someone called an agent who said she wanted to Take Dad Under Her Wing and Make Him Famous by selling his paintings all around the world. As if! Mum said that Dad's painting for the Exhibition had already been sold. And the agent said she'd sold the dismal picture of Hugo being the Mona Lisa. Suppose at least that means that neither of them will go on public display anywhere. But what kind of person would want a painting by my dad in their house? A painting that looks suspiciously like a member of my family?

first time he's let go of those paint brushes for AGES

looking even goofier than usual

*

118

ABSOLUTELY AMAZING AND ALMOST TOTALLY
IMPOSSIBLE THING TO BELIEVE (APART FROM THE FACT
THAT SOMEONE HAS PAID MONEY FOR A PAINTING BY
MY DAD):

My dad says he is going to buy himself a motorbike
with some of the money from his painting!!!!

Unbelievability Rating: At least 175 out of 10.

Is it possible that my dad is at last trying to be normal? Maybe even cool? Dad said he wants a Classic bike not some modern racing bike. Can he really want to buy a Harley Davidson? Imagine having a Harley parked outside our house!

MANIC MONDAY!
As if everything that happened on the Sunday wasn't bad enough, Monday came into my life and:

☻ *just about every teacher in school had seen the local paper and was going on about my dad*

☻ *Xanthe moped about the playground at break time and couldn't be cheered up even when I offered her my squashed fly pie at lunch*

☻ *had a double maths lesson*

☻ *Hugo tried to sit at a table only five tables away from me in the dining hall!*

☻ *My dad has already bought his motorbike*

☻ *My dad came to meet me from school on his motorbike*

☻ *My dad's motorbike is not a Harley Davidson*

☻ *I have never been as embarrassed in my whole entire life I was today (even the Circle of Love wasn't as bad as being picked up by my dad on his motorbike in front of my entire school).*

MOBILE PHONE FUND: *Pathetically still £5.61 (but am wondering if I can get something for the Euro if I take it to the bank).*

MY DAD'S A BIKER – AS IF!!!

Don't know which was the worst bit: the ancient World War Two motorbike complete with sidecar or the fact that Dad was wearing an old pair of rubber gloves, a pair of swimming goggles, his old holey wellies and a disgusting, smelly jacket. There wasn't a speck of leather in sight! So much for me thinking that there was a possibility that Dad just might be a bit cool.

Actually, the even worse worst bit could be that Tarquin was standing at the bus stop when we drove past.

My fanciability factor is now about minus 500. Could be even lower than that . . .

Have decided that I must do something to stop the continuous humiliation caused by my family. Consider the following options:

    1) leave home
    2) claim loss of memory and deny all knowledge of family
    3) commit mass murder of entire family
    4) difficult – actually can't think of a better plan
than 1), 2) and 3).

Have given lots of thoughts to above plans. Problem with 1) is, where would I go? Living on the streets would be even worse than living here. And, under the circumstances, I obviously couldn't go to Xanthe's. However, could go and live with Nono, which would be:

☆ v good idea because there would be lots of good scoff, lots of tellies, DVDs and telephones, always hot water for a bath and never Hugo's slimy things floating in the water, new things in the fridge, etc.

☆ bad idea because Mum and Dad would just come and fetch me to take me back here.

2) has possibilities but I am not sure I would be convincing enough to doctors for long enough to keep up loss of memory scam. Also a strong possibility that they would make me stay at home anyway and let Mum counsel me back to finding my memory.

3) could entail blood or other things that are Rather Nasty. Also seems a pretty drastic way of solving the problem and could end up in prison (worse again than living here, I bet) and don't think that being a mass murderess would make me feel v good.

Will have to find another plan.

Xanthe wasn't quite so fed up during the next few days. I did try to ask her how things were but she said she didn't really want to talk about it. Except she did say that her mum and dad weren't arguing much at the moment but that was mostly because they weren't speaking to each other at all.

Came home after school later in the week and found Mum and Dad in rather good mood. Dad was racing up and down the hallway again so began to wonder if he had sold another painting. Turned out that this new agent is taking

Mum and Dad to America because she thinks he is going to be famous and sell lots of paintings there. Do not think this can be true because we are talking about Dad here. But it is true that all Dad's paintings (except, of course, the murals on the walls) have been packed up like huge parcels and are sitting in the living room waiting to be sent to America.

Best news about Mum and Dad going to the States is that Nono is going to come and stay with us while they are away! Mum and Dad are going to America in two days' time.

NONO HAS STARTED TO HAVE HER THINGS BROUGHT OVER BY DAD. So far:

    ☆ loads of kitchen equipment (to make good things to eat)
    ☆ lots of wool and some knitting needles
    ☆ tons of magazines (I like it!)
    ☆ two suitcases.

Spoke to Nono on the phone and she says that she is also going to bring her mega widescreen telly, her DVD player, her Game Boy Advance and her PlayStation! But she won't bring them until the day Mum and Dad go away so that it is too late for them to complain about it.

Hugo has become even more painful than he was before. After the article in the newspaper about Dad's Exhibition painting and the cheesey photograph of Dad and Hugo in the same newspaper, Hugo thinks he is famous. He says that people are stopping him in the street and talking to him. Reckon people are stopping him in the street and talking to him because they think he has escaped from a zoo or something. My stinky brother now goes around looking at his reflection in mirrors and windows (anything with a shiny surface, in fact) and smiling back at himself. Cringe! Sadly cannot train Giggles to bite Hugo on the ankles because Giggles is almost certainly untrainable.

Xanthe thinks it's mildly cool to have a dad who's going to America to sell paintings.

She didn't want me to come back to hers after school — instead she came here. I gave her one of Nono's biscuits from the secret tin in my room. She stayed for ages and we tried out her new Superswirlcurl mascara. Xanthe looked gorgeous but I looked like I had a spider stuck to my cheek. In the end, Xanthe went home. I am probably the only nearly-teenager in the whole entire world who does not have a phone and therefore cannot send texts to my best friend who is feeling glum.

Mum and Dad have finally gone to America and Nono has moved in! First thing she did was to say, 'No, no,' and cover up Mum's portrait by the stairs.

We had all these things for tea:

- ☆ sausage rolls
- ☆ jam tarts
- ☆ chocolate cake
- ☆ Jaffa Cakes
- ☆ Tango AND Coke!!!!
- ☆ tinned tomato soup
- ☆ Quavers AND Wotsits!!!!!!!!!!!!!!
- ☆ spaghetti hoops in tomato sauce!

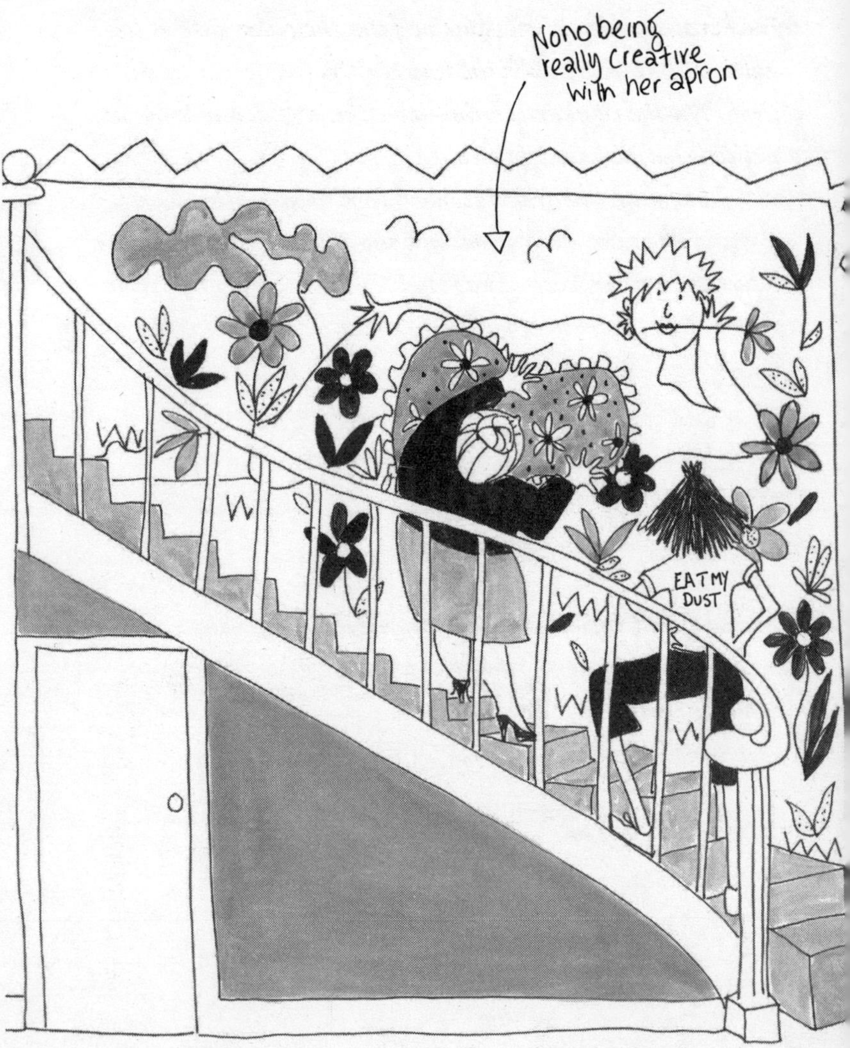

Nono being really creative with her apron
EAT MY DUST

Food is so good that Ben came up from the cellar to have tea with us! But then so did the rest of GOB (Nono calls them Geoffrey's string quartet). Gave Jake the evils. Don't think he noticed. Tarquin came to meet GOB because they were off to rehearse for another talent competition. Tarquin said that he thought my picture in the paper was good. He didn't mention Hugo's picture in the paper though! Hah!

yummy—
maker
extraordinaire

wish I had
two mouths

COOL

hope I've got
room for a bit
of this

the best
ever
Choccy
Cake

    Brian has taken over the living-room furniture. He sleeps on the sofa. Mum will go spare when she gets back. Giggles is having a nervous breakdown in the kitchen, although he does like the titbits that Nono gives him. Felt sorry enough for Giggles to give him a hug but he stinks so I am not sure I will do that again.

TOTAL HUMILIATION ON MY WAY HOME FROM SCHOOL TODAY! Was at the bus stop with Xanthe and Hugo was there too. Some complete stranger walked up to him and asked for his autograph because they had seen him in the paper! This is just too much!

MOBILE PHONE FUND: £7.61 (£2 from Nono for helping with washing-up).

MS PRETTY – MISTAKE!

Mum and Dad have made a BIG mistake! They have left Ben in charge of the shop while they are in America. Went in there on my way home with Xanthe.

All of GOB was in there, lying around thinking they looked cool. Puke machine Jake was there too. He still didn't say sorry and am beginning to wonder why I ever thought he was so great. Xanthe says that she always wondered but couldn't tell me that. Now she tells me!

Honestly, Ben is so useless he actually had Giggles in the shop! Dad always makes Giggles lie outside the shop because he smells. Dad also thinks that Giggles looks cute sitting outside the shop – like, right, Dad! He thinks that Giggles sitting outside the shop will make people want to come over and say, 'Hello, dear little friendly dog I must just come in and buy stuff'. Right

Xanthe and I went into the shop and no one even looked at us. No one said hello either. Except Frank – and I

131

*don't think I can even spell the words he said. Don't think
sailors are very polite if Frank's anything to go by. Was just
about to grab a bag of carob-coated nuts and raisins (carob is
not as nice as chocolate but it is the nearest thing to choccy
that Dad sells) and leave to go back to Nono when I NEARLY
DIED AND SO DID XANTHE! Ms Pretty, our fab drama
teacher from school, came in the shop! Ms Pretty:*

☆ always wears gorgeous clothes

☆ always smiles a kind of secret smile

☆ has extremely fabby shoes

☆ is my fave teacher

☆ does not talk to us like we are babies

☆ probably has a really cool boyfriend who is an actor or something.

Seemed to me that GOB were pretty gobsmacked by Ms Pretty when she came in. They all stood up! And Ben actually spoke!

He spoke! He did not grunt like he does to everyone else! Ms Pretty taught Ben at school too.

Ms Pretty bought loads of stuff. Hope she doesn't die of some kind of food poisoning as that would be just too embarrassing because Ms Pretty knows that my dad runs the shop. I know that because she spoke to me and told me. And she said she'd seen Dad in the paper and how proud I must be of him being so clever and so famous.

Began to wonder if Ms Pretty could honestly think that my dad is both clever and famous. Wondered if Ms Pretty was as smart as I thought. Decided she probably is because she has only spoken to my dad once, at a parents' evening. And it was only for five minutes anyway.

Then Ms Pretty went to leave the shop. TOTAL DISASTER! As she turned to go, Frank also turned round, lifted his tail feathers up and did a HUGE POO AND IT LANDED DOWN MS PRETTY'S BACK! Ms Pretty went

I've gone all hot and wobbly— why didn't Frank poo on JAKE?

home with parrot poo on her! She didn't seem to notice in the shop. Only Xanthe and I noticed. GOB wouldn't notice if they had parrot poo down their own backs. Actually, GOB wouldn't notice is Frank pooed down their fronts.

How can I go to school tomorrow if Frank has pooed down Ms Pretty? Told Ben and said he should do something about it. He just grunted a grunt which I think meant, 'Don't worry about it, it's only poo from a parrot'. Poo from a parrot is precisely something to worry about, though. Especially as the poo is down the back of my favourite teacher.

Xanthe said maybe the poo would have dropped off by the time she got home. Hope she is right. We left as soon as Ms Pretty had gone down the street. When Ben realized that we were going back home to have tea with Nono, he closed the shop. Dad will be v cross when he finds out Ben shut before five o'clock.

GOB followed us like a row of slugs all the way home. Tarquin wasn't with them, though.

Hugo Poogo was at home doing his homework already.
He isn't a slug, he is a toad! Just as Nono finished putting the
plates on the table, Hugo appeared in the kitchen and said he

137

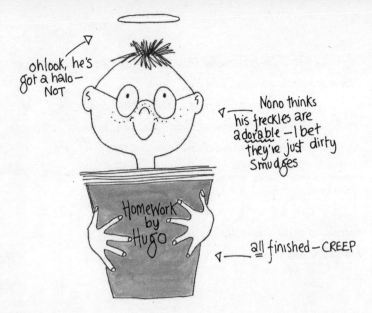

oh look, he's got a halo — NOT

Nono thinks his freckles are adorable — I bet they're just dirty smudges

Homework by Hugo

all finished — CREEP

had done all his homework and gave a big sucky uppy grin.
Nono told him he was a good boy and he didn't seem to mind!
Puke.

Good tea, though:

☆ two kinds of Swiss roll
☆ those marshmallow things covered in choc
with jam in the middle
☆ chips
☆ tomato sauce and HP sauce
☆ choc chip cookie CAKE!
☆ pizza with drizzly cheese
☆ chicken nuggets.

really scrummy greasy Chips

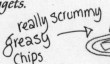

Nono does mind how much we pu on

Think GOB thought they could come back every day if Nono was going to cook like that. Huh!

Nono gave special food to Brian and Giggles too (she let Brian eat in the hallway). Giggles scoffed it quick but made terrible smells all evening. Stink!

Xanthe went home after tea. She said things were just the same at home. Poor Xanthe.

Did some of my homework. Would have sent text messages to all my mates if I had mobile phone. I might even have sent one to Tarquin too . . .

MOBILE PHONE FUND: still £7.61.

NEWS HORROR! MY COOL IS NOW TOTALLY BLOWN!

Watched telly with Nono. Living room much improved by arrival of Surround Sound Megawide Home Cinema telly of Nono's. Perhaps my newly famous father will be rich enough to buy one for us when he gets back from America. Like, right! Just saw a pig fly past the window too . . .

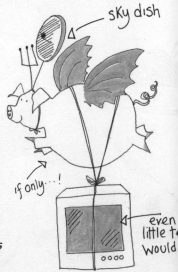

sky dish

if only...!

even little t
would

GOB were rehearsing in the cellar. Mum and Dad don't let them do that but Nono doesn't seem to mind. With the Surround Sound you can't hear GOB anyway — which is a relief. Even after the wedding, Nono still seems

140

to think that GOB is a group of musicians like one of those string quartets.

Anyway, when the news started on the telly, Nono said we needed to put the cover on Dad's bike.

I said, 'What cover? Dad doesn't cover it up.'

She said, 'I know but I've knitted a nice cover to protect it.'

Nono knits all the time but even I didn't know that Nono could knit covers for bikes. She said she'd made it out of oddments of wool that she had left over. There must have been a lot of oddments because she pulled this huge thing out

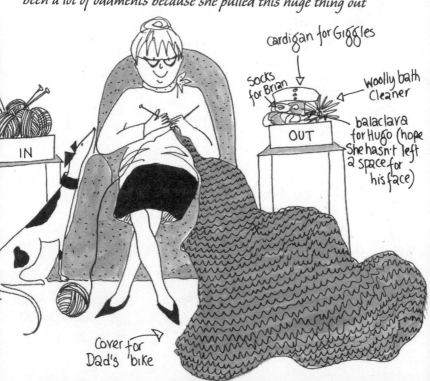

fashionable Frank— NoT!

Giggles needs therapy

Knitted hairband

cardigan for Giggles

Socks for Brian

Woolly bath Cleaner

OUT

balaclava for Hugo (hope she hasn't left a space for his face)

IN

Cover for Dad's bike

of her knitting bag and asked me to help her put it over the bike. Good job it was getting dark and no one could see us.

Like, right! Dad parks his bike thingy in the front garden and Nono and I were just putting this jumper cover over it when Tarquin popped up from the cellar cover. Didn't even know he was down there in the first place. He gave Nono a fright and she jumped backwards. Tarquin caught her and said he was really sorry and could he help. Nono giggled and kept calling him 'such a kind boy'.

Anyway, between us we managed to get the cover on the bike. Got to hand it to Nono. It may have been a pretty weird idea to knit a cover for a motorbike and side car but she made it really well and it was a perfect fit. But then she said

nice pom pom

why is H here ag

she had to rush inside. Like, why? And she left me with Tarquin on the door step. It was so embarrassing!!!

Tarquin said, 'Nice bike.'

And I said, 'Like, yeah!'

Then he said, 'But it is a nice bike, it's a collector's item,' and he went on to say how it was actually a really cool bike to have and he'd rather ride one of those than a Harley any day.

Was he for real? Did he really mean that? After all, he knows my dad and he must know that my dad so isn't cool. Is he?

We stood and chatted for a bit but then the rest of GOB came up from the cellar and we couldn't talk any more. Jake didn't even look at me. Like I said, I hate Jake and I don't know why I ever liked him. He is a disgusting puke machine. And he can't play music. Or sing.

Jake asked Tarquin if he wanted a lift home in the GOB van. He said no he'd follow in a minute.

We chatted a bit more, me and Tarquin. It was OK. He made me laugh a lot. He's actually really funny. (Ha ha — not funny peculiar.) Then Tarquin said, 'Tell you what. Give me your mobile number and I'll send you one of those picture things of a motorbike.'

It was dead embarrassing! I didn't know what he meant about 'picture things' and I am still the only person in the entire universe (apart from my parents) who hasn't got a mobile phone! Had to tell him that.

He said 'never mind' and then he showed me on his

phone. It was cool! Turned out that those picture things are pictures you make out of letters and numbers. Not bad!

When he was leaving, Tarquin said, 'See you at school then.'

And I said, 'OK.'

Did I say the right thing? Should I have said 'maybe'? I am so nearly thirteen and I still don't know what you are meant to say to boys who aren't your smelly brothers (and in my case both VERY smelly). I must be the only girl in the world of my age who is hopeless with boys.

Went back inside. Nono was watching the telly and knitting something else. Don't know what it was but it was going to be purple and fluffy. Ben was slobbed out. Brian was sitting next to Nono on the big armchair watching the telly. Hugo was pretending to read a book and not watch the telly but I know he was watching it really. He is such a liar.

I had to sit on a cushion on the floor – great! But the Surround Sound made me feel better – after all, we had to make the most of it before Mum and Dad got back.

Nono is really cool. She doesn't seem to know about bedtimes and stuff like that. She just goes to bed when she's tired. Anyway, we watched this programme about police and then all the soaps (didn't know the storylines on any of them on account of the fact that we can't usually watch them, but that didn't seem to matter too much). Then, later, we were watching the evening news when I thought I was going to DIE.

There was the news lady all smiley reading out the bad things that had happened in our area when she said something about exciting news from America about a local painter. And then it showed MY MUM AND MY DAD SHAKING HANDS WITH THE AMERICAN PRESIDENT AND A WHOLE LOAD OF OTHER PEOPLE IN SUITS!! AND my mum has done something kind of trendy with her hair! Even Ben sat up when Mum and Dad were on the telly and Hugo practically sat on Nono's lap — creep! Giggles started to howl, so we didn't manage to hear all of it — even with the Surround Sound. But we did hear that my dad's been asked to paint the President because they said Dad was one of the greatest painters of the century! As if! Are they mad? Can only think they are saying that because the century has only just started. There will be loads more painters loads better than my dad by the end of it!

he's on T.V. wearing THAT HAT??

What's happened to her hair??

the President of the U.S.A. — shame he's got dandruff on his collar..

Nono's really pleased — I WISH I WAS DEAD

Nono has stopped knitting for a moment

Nono said she felt quite faint and had to go to bed.
Ben said he'd stay up and watch some late film on
the telly.

THIS CANNOT BE TRUE!!!

Hugo went up to bed but I
saw him doing posey things in front of
the mirror in the bathroom. Reckon he
thinks he's going to be in one of Dad's next
paintings. Perlease!

I went to bed but couldn't sleep. Had too
many things to think about before going to school the next day:

🔦 still don't have mobile phone and only £7.61 towards
buying one

🔦 don't know what to say to Tarquin if I see him

🔦 what if I see Tarquin and he doesn't say anything to me?

🔦 don't know how to make Xanthe realize that

146

everything will be OK

    💡 Hugo and Ben are still my brothers

    💡 think my mother may have a new haircut that is too young for her

    💡 other people will have watched the news and seen my dad

    💡 my family is just too embarrassing

    💡 wondering if Nono is knitting my birthday present

    💡 only a few weeks before my birthday and I still haven't arranged my party.

MOBILE PHONE FUND: Deeply depressing . . .

CAN MY LIFE GET MUCH WORSE THAN THIS?

Have to make my own brekkie when Mum and Dad are here (really chewy bowl of Dad's muesli with extra gritty bits) but when Nono's around you get a decent fry-up. Hugo Poogo goes all wimpy and says things like, 'Oh no, Nono, we mustn't or our bodies will clog up with nasty things.' But I notice that he still eats the scrummy waffles, toast, fried bread and eggs that Nono puts in front of him. Hah!

School was a nightmare. Thought I'd got away with not many people seeing Dad on telly last night but oh, no. Mr Fat Face Headmaster only had to go and tell THE WHOLE SCHOOL IN THE MIDDLE OF ASSEMBLY!

I'm like, HELP! Don't do this, Mr Headmaster. SIR!

And he's like, 'Isn't this marvellous? Two of our very own students! Their father a famous painter! Painting the

President of America!'
    He said it like it was some big deal. He also said it like it's true that my dad is a famous painter. Get real, everyone! My dad just paints pictures in the living room — he's going to get found out dead soon.

WORSE. The headmaster made me and Hugo stand up in front of the whole school. As if they didn't know who we were. Tried to pretend I wasn't there and made an attempt to hide behind Xanthe's rucksack but oh, no. Dear, sweet, baby brother (who I am going to murder as soon as I get the chance) went and stood up all grinny faced and pointed me out! Then everyone laughed at me.

EVEN WORSE. Tarquin was standing at the back of the school hall when I left. He was with his mates but he still smiled at me. And he said, 'Hi!'

Why does he always have to see the most embarrassing bits of my life?

I'm even too upset to roll up my skirt

What did he mean? Asked Xanthe and she said he probably just meant hello. But Tarquin is a boy so it can't be as simple as that, surely?

Saw Tarquin again in the lunch queue. He asked me if I wanted some chips and when I said yes he put them on my plate. Then he said he'd seen the news last night and thought it was pretty cool to have a dad who was going to paint the President of America. Wonder if it is?

Got home from school and Mrs Baxter from next door was there with all her dogs. Got to admit, some of her Baxter terriers aren't that bad. But, on the other hand, some are that bad — like the ones that have the really dodgy-looking eyes or tails that are twice as long as their bodies. There was even one once that looked as though it was growing a third ear. Creepy.

I think Mrs Baxter might be bald and this fringe is attached to her headscarf

BONIO

Brian, modeling this season's knitwear collection

small but stinky

Mum had sent us a postcard from America. She'd
written it like a poem . . .

Here I am
(without my babies)
In the States
I won't catch rabies!

Statue of Liberty
There when it needs to be
Empire State Building
How homesick I'm feeling . . .

Papa is famous!
The paintings he's made — yes!
Are lining the walls
In Hallowed Halls.

Will be home soon!
My love — it has flown
Across the water
To my sons and daughter.

Send good wishes to Nono
Don't spend hours on the phone — no!
Keep Brian off the sofa
And don't be out late, huh?

Love, Mum xxx

Not a lot to say really.

Giggles was sitting in the corner of the kitchen sulking even more than usual on account of all those terriers. Brian was just being Brian. Nono had been busy knitting again. Whilst she'd been watching the shopping channel on telly all morning she had knitted the American flag, complete with all its stars and stripes. She said she wanted to put it on Dad's bike for when he got home. Actually it looks quite cool because she's used some sparkly wool for the starry bits. She's still knitting though – this time she is going to make coats for all Mrs Baxter's terriers. Some of them have bald patches, you see.

Mrs Baxter and Nono were having a great time chatting away. They carried on talking while we put the tea on the table (usual scrummy scoff). Hugo, little toad, was of course about to go off to do his homework instead of watching telly. (Nono brought her portable telly for the kitchen as well.) Then Mrs Baxter said that she'd brought me and Hugo something special. It was a big bottle of lemonade. Mrs Baxter handed it over with a bit of a wink. She seems to know that things like lemonade are only allowed when Nono is around. Hugo said he couldn't possibly drink it because it would rot his teeth.

Xanthe did my hair with her curling tongs during science →

I think Hugo is:

- stupid
- a creep
- awful
- rude
- cringeworthy
- about to be tripped up on the stairs so that he bangs his head and hurts it!

Told Mrs Baxter that I loved lemonade and if Hugo wasn't going to drink his, I would drink it instead.

△ Well, if Hugo Poogo doesn't want his, I'll have to drink

POP

Ben hangs around the house loads more when Nono is here. Think it is because of:

- ☆ the food
- ☆ the telly
- ☆ the food
- ☆ the Game Boy
- ☆ the food
- ☆ the PlayStation
- ☆ the food

Unfortunately GOB also hang around a lot more too. Have decided to give Jake the evils every time I see him now. When he sees how long my hair is going to grow and how gorgeous it is going to be, he will be dead sorry that he puked on my trainers. When I am interviewed after my debut live solo on Top of the Pops, I will tell everyone about those trainers!

waving to my fans on Top of the Pops

really long hair and HUGE eyelashes

lots of rings

total babe

Mum and Dad rang after we had eaten. Nono told them that we had seen them on the telly and Mum just giggled. (I could hear because Nono has got this special cordless phone that acts as a second handset and she brought it with her to our house.) Mum said they'd been to loads of parties and had bought lots of stuff. I'm like — what? I mean, my mum and dad don't go to parties! They are too old and too embarrassing to go to parties!

AWFUL THOUGHT! Mum and Dad might have tried to dance at these parties. That means American people have seen their pathetic attempts at dancing.

Still trying to get my head round fact that Mum has been shopping. What kind of shopping? Perhaps they have bought great presents from American shops! Perhaps they have bought me:

☆ Skecher trainers in metallic pink
☆ some Calvins
☆ a Polo jumper
☆ engineered Levi's
☆ CKOne

Maybe they have bought me some seriously good birthday presents? Will find out in two days' time when they are coming home. Good thing about them coming home will be the presents. Bad things will be:

- not being able to stay up late
- good food will only be available at Nono's again
- Nono will have to take all her tellies and things away

BUT maybe Mum and Dad will have seen the tellies in America and now buy one for us.

sparkly back pack

designer smellies

Clompy, cloggy fab coloured shoes

GUCCI

Jelly beans

make up – natch

inflatable bra (just until I don't need the air)

Somehow I doubt it . . .

MOBILE PHONE FUND: £8.11 (Mrs Baxter gave me 50p 'to buy some sweets' when she left).

FAMOUS PAINTER RETURNS HOME NOT WEARING HIS SANDALS

Xanthe was really quiet at school all day. Told her about my mum and dad dancing in public in America and she said at least they were together and having a good time. Felt a bit stupid after that. But Xanthe agreed to come back to ours after school for one of Nono's teas.

That was when she told me. Xanthe's dad's gone. For ever. Her mum and dad have split up! I can't believe it.

They always seemed so perfect. Just like all those people in magazines! But Xanthe says that actually they've been fighting for so long like they hate each other that she can't remember when it was really good any more. Xanthe says her mum doesn't even do much with her jewellery stuff at the moment either. And her dad has told her that now that her mum and dad aren't together, they'll actually be able to be happy. She said he'd actually said that they'd all be happy if they lived apart.

Looking at Xanthe, it didn't seem like it could be true to me. Fat lot her dad knew about being happy, if you ask me.

Nono was brill! She gave Xanthe a hug and said that even if it seemed really awful at the moment, it would get better in the end. Nono says that everything gets better in the end. She said even Xanthe's mum would feel better one day. Don't know how Nono knows things like that, but I know she was telling the truth. Nono never lies and she would never make someone believe something that she didn't think would happen.

Xanthe seemed to be feeling better after Nono spoke to her. Glad Nono was there because not sure I would have been any good. Good thing was, though, that when GOB arrived, Nono seemed to know that Xanthe wouldn't want them there with us. She sent them down into Ben's pit with loads of scoff. They went with a grunt — actually it was lots of grunts because they were obviously feeling pleased with the food. Tarquin wasn't with them though. Then Nono gave Hugo some sandwiches and chocolate cake and he went upstairs to do his homework without being asked. SAD BOY!

Gosh! Xanthe's mum looks even sadder than Xanthe

Nono knitted this ou of old tights —

When Xanthe's mum came to get her, Nono sent me and Xanthe to watch the telly while she had a cup of tea with her. Don't know what she said to Xanthe's mum but she was looking a bit more cheerful when she and Xanthe left.

I LOVE NONO FOR MAKING EVERYONE AND EVERYTHING BETTER.

Went home straight after school the next day. Only just had time to change before there was a taxi outside the house. The hallway was FULL OF SHOPPING BAGS within minutes. Mum and Dad were back from America! Know this will sound pathetic but I was quite pleased to see them. Not a huge amount but a bit.

Hugo was just so lightweight! He did all this sucky uppy stuff and threw himself at Mum and said things like, 'It is so good to see you, Mother dearest I have missed you so.' Perlease!

My parents looked different from when they left. A lot different:

MUM:

☆ was wearing different earrings. Still dangly but not quite so dangly and not so obvious really

☆ had different coloured hair

☆ had shiny hair

☆ had new glasses on. And they say Ralph Lauren on the frame!

☆ had make up on!

☆ was wearing clothes that weren't as baggy as usual.

DAD:

☆ was wearing a Hawaiian shirt!

☆ was wearing one of Nono's sleeveless jumpers — but this was made from sparkly wool

☆ was wearing Docksider shoes!

☆ still wasn't wearing any socks though

☆ was wearing a new beret

☆ had a goatee beard instead of his usual face fungus!

Mum and Dad seemed pleased to be home. Ben came up from the cellar and grunted at them. Then he slumped in one of the kitchen chairs. Nono had made a cake and iced it with the American flag. It was that kind of frosty icing stuff because Nono said it was American icing. And she'd done the stars on the cake (the stars that are on the flag, I mean) out of those little sugary silver balls. It was cool. Normally Mum and Dad would go bonkers about us eating food like that. They'd moan about:

- the sugar
- the artificial colouring
- the e numbers

But they didn't say anything and just ate it like the rest of us! And they didn't say anything about Nono having a telly in the kitchen. Or Frank wearing a jumper.

In fact, Mum and Dad just talked and talked! They told us all about some exhibition of Dad's paintings that was held in a gallery and how all these people came to a special party there. Mum kept on mentioning names of singers and movie stars who had been at the party. Like, right! Like my mum actually knows the names of real singers and movie stars! NOT.

Then Dad came out with all this stuff about feeling that his art had been understood for the first time. What kind of rubbish is that? They're just paintings, aren't they? That's all. But Dad said that painting the President's portrait had

165

been good. And he said that other people had asked him to paint pictures for them and that his agent was going to fly Mum and Dad out to America again later in the year.

Am I in some kind of weird dream? If I am not:

☆ hope that next trip to America is during the summer holidays so that we can all go
☆ that we get to stay in a hotel
☆ that we can go to Disneyland.

Actually, maybe we could stay in a big house in Beverley Hills with a swimming pool instead.

moi in Disneyland — I wish . . . .

MICKY

MOBILE PHONE FUND: *Too depressing to think about . . .*

MY MUM WENT TO AMERICA
AND MY BROTHER GOT
THE T-SHIRT!

Took a while for Mum and Dad to get the message that we weren't that interested in finding out what the President had said to them. What we wanted to know was what was in those carrier bags!

Nono, who is a genius, had it sussed. She said, 'Let me make us all another cup of tea and then we can go into the living room to see all the lovely new clothes you've bought.' And Mum fell for it.

I, being another genius, had Hugo sussed because I then said, 'Let me carry the bags in for you.'

Hugo, being such a creep and not a genius, said, 'Oh, I'll carry them.' And he did! All of them. Ha ha!

Gucci, Prada, Armani, Giorgio and Ferragamo bags
were sadly lacking. However, there were some tempting ones
that said things like Big Brown Bag and Woof!

We all settled down in the living room (Hugo had to
sit with Giggles) and waited to see what was going to happen.

First, Mum showed us some of her things. Actually they weren't too bad, although I am not at all sure about the stripy trousers. Still, at least the stripes weren't going round her and went up and down instead.

elastic bit for when she eats too much

Zip at side-weird

mum's new trousers

Dad had about ten Hawaiian shirts in all sorts of colours. I suppose he thinks they are trendy or something. SAD! So, yawn, yawn, we looked at all those things and then we had to say nice things about some weird salad bowl and servers that Mum had bought. Oh — and then she produced a pizza slicer. Like we've never seen a pizza slicer before! Sad thing is, I don't think Mum realizes that:

smart labels

Wonder if she'll paint her toe nails

heels!! – almost

ant

🔮 you can get them here
and
🔮 she never lets us have pizza anyway!

THOUGHT: Perhaps now Mum has been to America she thinks it is OK to cook pizza!

Nono got her present first. It was an apron. An apron! My mum and dad went all the way to America and all they could bring back for Nono was AN APRON!!! Too sad. And Mum was so pleased with herself too! Because the apron had this cutesy kitten on the front and, when you pressed it, the kitten went, 'Miaow!' Mum wasn't quite so pleased with herself when Giggles showed an unusual amount of energy and leaped up to attach his teeth to the kitten.

Ben was next. He got one of those T-shirts that said, 'My Mum and Dad Went to America and All I Got Was This Lousy T-shirt'. Ben gave two grunts, so I think that means that he likes it.

Hugo had this great big box and inside were some Skechers! I was just thinking, 'This is so not fair!' when I wondered whether, if Hugo had those, I had:

☆ something better
   or
☆ a pair of Skechers for me!

Thought things were looking up — except Hugo is so thick I don't think he realized how cool his present was. Come to think of it, don't think Mum and Dad realized either.

I don't think Ben wants people to know he's got a mum and Dad (me neither)

MY MUM + DAD WENT TO AMERICA + ALL I GOT IS THIS LOUSY T-SHIRT

TYPICAL! Poogoo gets a really decent present

at least ggles is uying ng this on

FUZZY'S USA

Then Mum gave me this great big carrier bag that said 'Parapluie' on the side. It looked promising. Then I found out what was inside. It . . . It . . . IT WAS DISGUSTING!

OK, so Nono got a dodgy plastic apron that makes noises but Ben got a T-shirt, which was not too bad, and Hugo got cool trainers.

What did I get?

A transparent plastic rain cape with flashing bits and this hood thing that looks like an umbrella!

Like, yum, yum, kiss, kiss! NOT! To make it even worse — it was orange! Mum and Dad said they chose that colour because it reminded them of Auntie Melissa's wedding and the 'lovely dress' that I had to wear.

Had thought that maybe this was some kind of joke and that any minute now they would give me another bag with my real present in it. NOT! Had to sit there wearing it while the other things were unpacked. Ben laughed at me! Haven't heard Ben laugh for years so I must look really bad.

I sat and sulked on the sofa but nobody noticed. Even Giggles got a better present than me. He got some knot thing that Dad said was made out of indestructible doggie dental floss. Giggles barked at it at first. Then he got down to the business of ripping it apart. He did a good job and I wished I could do the same to my Fanta cape.

bandana

dental floss

looking really pleased

I expect he'll eat the box once he's finished the floss

Dad gave Brian a bandana to wear round his neck. The fabric was decorated with the American flag. Nono was really pleased. Brian looked pleased too. Frank got a water bowl that plays the American National Anthem every time he drinks from it. He seemed to think it was really weird at first and he sat in his cage with his head tilted to one side looking cross. Then he

he makes enough noise without this

Frank'll need tranquillizers later

took a drink from it, flew up on to his perch and screamed, 'Pop! Get the gun!' at the top of his voice. Weird.

Went round to Xanthe's after that. Had to show her how awful my present was. Xanthe was looking dead mizz. Xanthe's mum was lying on the sofa when I got there. She was playing 'All By Myself' on the CD player. Xanthe said she'd played some desperate country-and-western song called 'D-I-V-O-R-C-E' all morning. And she'd been watching some film on cable about a woman dying of a terminal illness.

You could actually feel the sadness in Xanthe's house. It was awful.

I can hardly bear to touch this, this THING

Visor with windscreen wiper

she seems to be so sad

Joked with Xanthe about the rain cape and that made her smile a bit. She wasn't laughing at me though. She just kind of knew how rubbish it was. Like best friends do. Like I

174

know it is for Xanthe at the moment. Managed to make her actually laugh when I told her what Frank had said. We wondered where Frank had learned it and why he'd never said it before.

Bumped into Tarquin on the way out. I wanted to stop and chat with him but I just couldn't think of what to say. So I didn't say anything. Why? DISASTER!

Had loads of homework. Did some and then I couldn't concentrate any more. Thought about Xanthe a lot. I mean, my family are nutters but at least my mum and dad still talk to each other and spend time with each other. Even if they did buy me an orange plastic rain cape with flashing lights and an umbrella hood. For some reason I kept thinking about Tarquin as well . . .

THINGS WRONG WITH MY LIFE:

- my family (all nutters except for Nono)
- our dog smells
- our parrot says rude things
- my aunt has married a complete pencil case with hairy bits
- my true talents are not being appreciated
- no mobile!
- Jake puked on my best trainers (actually my only trainers!)
- Xanthe being so desperate and there is not much I can do about it
- too shy to talk to Tarquin

THINGS OK WITH MY LIFE:

   ☆ *my best friend is Xanthe*

   ☆ *Nono*

   ☆ *school gets me away from Ben (how sad is that?)*

   ☆ *Tarquin's being nice to me*

   ☆ *have my own bedroom*

   ☆ *can't think of anything else! HOW SAD IS THAT?*

PARTY PARTY!

I am going to be thirteen at the end of the week and no one in my family seems to have noticed! Don't think they realize how important my birthday is! Absolutely everyone else at school has a HUGE party for their thirteenth birthday with loads of presents, people and food.

As no one else seems to have thought about my birthday, have decided to plan my own party. It will be:

- ☆ *eight till late!*
- ☆ *come as your favourite Pop Idol*
- ☆ *a karaoke disco*
- ☆ *somewhere big like the community hall so that everyone can come*

AND:

- ☆ *it will have a big table for all my presents*

Have done the invitation:

THINGS I WOULD LIKE FOR MY PRESENTS:

- ☆ mobile
- ☆ Armani jeans
- ☆ Chanel duffle bag
- ☆ Gucci belt
- ☆ Prada T-shirt
- ☆ Pucci print shirt
- ☆ vouchers for my mobile
- ☆ subscription to Vogue magazine
- ☆ subscription to Cosmo Girl magazine
- ☆ ten skirts from New Look
- ☆ American baseball jacket
- ☆ hair extensions
- ☆ fake tattoo (a real one would really hurt!)
- ☆ fake belly-button ring (a real one would really, really hurt!)
- ☆ loads of money
- ☆ CD player and loads of CDs
- ☆ DVD player and loads of DVDs
- ☆ mobile cover
- ☆ loads of bubble bath
- ☆ my own set of fluffy towels
- ☆ Hugo to be adopted by another family
- ☆ one of those cute little motorbikes to go to school on

Chances of getting any of these things: about two out of ten.

Took list downstairs to Mum and Dad as a subtle hint. Thought I'd better not put any more things on the list in case they felt I was being greedy.

HONESTLY! My family are the pits! Mum and Dad said I couldn't have a party in the community hall because it would be too big and not a family occasion. That's exactly what I want it to be! DO NOT WANT TO HAVE A PARTY WITH HUGO THERE! Do not want to have Ben there either because he will probably bring GOB and that means Jake too. And he might puke all over my new Armani jeans! My family do not understand anything.

Now Mum and Dad say that they are doing a party for me and they had wanted it to be a surprise. Oh, really?

Mum says that I am not allowed in the kitchen except for meal times. I said, 'Good — that means I can't help with the cooking or do the washing-up'. And she said, 'Oh no it doesn't!'
It is just so not fair.

Told Mum that I would write a list of the people that I wanted to come to my non-surprise surprise party. She said she'd already invited everyone that she knew I would want to come. Like right. Hope Nono has seen the list because it will be better if she has seen it.

spoon makes a really good microphone

tinsel tiara

chopped off T-shirt customized by ME

frilly pants over jeans, very now

Star

finally painted flowers on my shoes

Went up to my room to practise singing like a popstar. Then I had a go at text messaging. Hard without the phone but I wrote them down:

Ttl Bab CLng (think that means Total Babe Calling)
C U 2Nite 8 (see you tonight at eight)
C U At PrtE (see you at the party)

C U L8r (see you later)
Mite B 3 (might be free)
Othng 2 ? (nothing to wear)
COl! (cool)

Wasn't sure what else to text about. Would have phoned Xanthe to ask her but couldn't because the house was full of people. Now that Nono has gone home we're back to only one phone in the hallway. And Dad spends all his time painting in the living room and gets Ben to work in the shop during the week still. Hugo is trying to make an ant hill in the garden and Mum is letting him because she says it is harmless and educational. She won't say that when she gets ants in her new American sandals.

MOBILE PHONE FUND: £10.11 (Nono gave me £2 when she went home).

AT LAST I AM A TEENAGER!

Today was my party. It is official — I AM A TEENAGER! I have had cards from:

☆ *Mum and Dad*
☆ *Ben and Hugo (almost certainly bought by Mum but just about signed by them)*
☆ *Nono*
☆ *Xanthe*
☆ *Auntie Melissa, Doug and her Bump (honestly — that's what she wrote! Disgusting!)*
☆ *six friends at school*
☆ *Mrs Baxter*
☆ *Giggles, Frank and Brian (another card from Nono really)*

That makes thirteen cards for thirteen years!
School was OK because I am no longer one of the little

kids. Xanthe gave me these really gorgeous bracelets at school. All spangly and lots of them. I want to wear them all the time.

doing her best to be happy

lovely sparkly paper

they make this amazing tinkly noise

My 'secret' party was this afternoon. Like, do my parents actually realize that I am thirteen and not three? Like, NOT! My 'secret' guests were:

- Mum
- Dad
- Xanthe
- Nono
- Ben
- Hugo
- Giggles
- Brian
- Frank
- Auntie Melissa
- Doug

Some surprise! There was no one else from school there because Mum said she thought, 'I'd prefer to keep it quiet and intimate'. And I thought telling her I wanted to have a karaoke disco would have been a bit of a hint.

So, instead of a disco, I had a tea party in the kitchen, just like some little kid would.

Mum had decorated the kitchen with balloons — cringe! And she'd made things like jelly. Course, the jelly was from Dad's shop so it didn't have any colouring, any sugar or anything artificial. Didn't have any taste either!

Thankfully Nono arrived with bags full of stuff. She'd made some cakes and things — so at least some of the scoff was edible. And she'd made my birthday cake. It was dead cool! It was shaped like a handbag and had all these things hanging out of it.

There was:

- ☆ a fun camera
- ☆ a tiny Walkman
- ☆ a groovy purse
- ☆ hair mascara
- ☆ nail decorations
- ☆ money!
- ☆ chewing gum

Then Nono gave me another present — all wrapped up in silver tissue paper. It was a Prada T-shirt! Nono is just brilliant!

She knew exactly what I wanted. But breathtaking news! She also gave me a mobile phone! A real one! And Nono had put £20 on it. I love her more than ever.

Mum and Dad gave each other a Look. One of those 'For Heaven's sake' ones. They gave Nono a Look too — but she just smiled sweetly as if she didn't understand what the Look meant. Mum and Dad can't take the phone away from me now, can they? Nono gave it to me.

Just then Auntie Melissa arrived with Doug (Mum says I should call him Uncle Doug — NO WAY!) and that was

so not what I wanted. Not for my birthday party anyway. They gave me my present. It was a wooden pencil case that Doug had made. Auntie Melissa had painted it with flowers – like the ones on their long boat. Didn't really know what to say. It was the sort of pencil case that I had at primary school but the flowers were OK. They didn't even give me any gel pens to keep in it!

Course, Ben didn't give me anything at all. Hugo, however, gave me a chrysalis. Like, what am I meant to do with that? Mum and Dad seemed to think it was a really cool present.

Mum said, 'Oh, it'll turn into a beautiful butterfly.'

So what? I can't send a text with it – BUT I CAN WITH MY MOBILE!

Then Dad gave me his present. It was one of his paintings. Of me as a baby! He seemed really pleased with it and I'm like, 'Thanks, Dad.' He and Doug had made the frame out of wood they'd found in the canal. So cool. So not what I wanted.

Last present was from Mum. Now that was a surprise. It was a pair of jeans. When I opened the parcel they looked really promising. Mum was pleased with herself because she said they were a designer label and she knew I wanted a pair of them. They looked so cool. Then I saw the label. ARMINI.

Nono squeezed my hand. She knew. Xanthe gave me a look. She knew too. But Mum didn't . . . and she never would.

So I went with Xanthe to my room and changed into the Prada T-shirt and the Armini jeans and all of Xanthe's bracelets. Not bad. But the mobile's better!

Actually the 'designer' label is quite good. If I am careful, no one will notice.

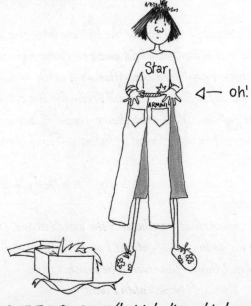

◁— oh!

MOBILE PHONE FUND: £10.11 (but I don't need to buy a mobile any more because I've already got one!).

CAN MY LIFE GET ANY BETTER THAN THIS?

Went back down to the kitchen in my new outfit with Xanthe. Mum and Dad had given everyone paper hats to wear. Even Frank had one. After we'd eaten — but before we got to eat my cake — Doug said, 'Now for the entertainments', and he put on a black cape (home-made of course — probably from something he'd found in the canal) and started waving a magic wand.

Mum said, 'Isn't it lovely, Uncle Doug is going to do some magic?'

I looked at Xanthe and she looked at me. Doug wanted to use me as his assistant but I said, 'No way — it's my birthday. I think Hugo would be much better.'

Course, Hugo couldn't wait!

I made a wish that Doug's magic would work and he could make Hugo disappear for real.

But what did I care? I'VE GOT A MOBILE!

Don't know how long Doug has been practising as a magician but he's not very good at it. He kept waving his hands about and saying, 'Wazoo, wazoom.' What does that mean? His first trick was trying to turn a cup of water upside down without the water falling out. It didn't work and he managed to pour the water all over Giggles, who bit him. Dad tried to make Giggles go into the garden but he wouldn't go.

Then Doug did a trick with Frank. Think Doug should have known better but he waved his cloak all over Frank's cage and made him disappear . . . only he didn't because suddenly Frank shrieked, 'Take that,' and pecked Doug really hard in the armpit. (He'd tried hiding him under his jumper.) Think it hurt!

Ben started to laugh. So he's still alive! It was the only noise he'd made since the party had begun because he was too busy eating Nono's food.

After the thing with Frank, Nono said, 'Let's cut the cake.'

Dad lit the candles and I made another wish before blowing them out.

I wished that I had Tarquin at my party. Oh well.

But the cake did taste good anyway. Very good.

Followed Xanthe to the door when she had to go. Nono gave her a hug. Think she appreciated that. She still looks sad but she said her dad was coming round for supper. She was looking forward to seeing him and so was her mum. Hope it goes OK.

I was on the doorstep saying goodbye, wishing her luck
with her mum and dad, when Tarquin came up the road.

I told him GOB weren't in the cellar and he said, 'I
know.'

'So what are you doing here?' I said.

'I came to see you.'

I'm like, WOW! My birthday wish had come true!

Xanthe said, 'It's her birthday today.'

Tarquin said, 'I know – that's why I'm here!'

He did? It was? Had this really strange, new feeling. It was kind of fluttery.

I felt really dumb, though, because I couldn't think of anything to say to him — again!

Xanthe winked at me, said, 'See you later', and left.

It's for ME!

I'm, like, standing on the doorstep with Tarquin. Then he said, 'I got you this,' and he gave me a present.

It was all wrapped up in spangly cellophane stuff. It looked really fabby. I dived in and unwrapped it. It was a cover for my mobile. It had all these jewels on it. WICKED!

I said, 'It's great. Thanks!' and felt like a twit. Then I

said, 'How did you know I'd got a mobile for my birthday?'

Tarquin said Nono had told him! I wanted to tell Tarquin it was just fantastic, fabby, brilliant, the best present I've ever been given (apart from the mobile itself, of course). But I couldn't speak because I felt so fluttery still.

Then Ben popped his head up from the cellar and looked at us both. Jake pulled up in the GOB van. Tarquin said, 'Well, I'd better go.' And that was it.

The party was really over then and I went up to my room. I just stood there looking at my phone. It is so cool! Wondered if Tarquin buying me the cover means that he likes me?

Read the book on how to use the mobile and wanted to send a text to Xanthe. Only I couldn't because I didn't know her number. Now I'd got a phone, I couldn't text or ring anyone because I didn't know anyone else's number on account of being the last person in the world to get a mobile!

Decided to go downstairs to ask if Mum and Dad knew Nono's number. At least I could send a text to her. But then suddenly my phone went BEEP BEEP. Someone had sent me a message! Couldn't work out how I could have got a message when no one else knew I had a mobile.

It was from Tarquin. It said CN I C U? Like he needed to ask? Sent a message back — YES! — and we are going to McDonald's on Saturday!!! What a brilliant birthday!

BAD THINGS ABOUT BEING THIRTEEN:

☻ *still have brother called Ben and another one called Hugo*

☻ *my bedroom looks like a baby's*

☻ *will have new cousin soon and think my family thinks that I will be able to babysit one day*

☻ *my dad wears Hawaiian shirts and thinks he is a cool painter*

☻ *my mum thinks my dad is cool*

☻ *have got some lousy presents but have written all over new pencil case with my (old) gel pens: A & T 4 EVA!*

GOOD THINGS ABOUT BEING THIRTEEN:

☆ *have mobile!*

☆ *have best friend called Xanthe*

☆ *have cool new outfit*

☆ *think I might have a boyfriend!*

☆ *mobile has cool cover*

☆ *got a date on Saturday*

☆ *if my dad really is going to be famous, I might start to get better presents.*

MOBILE PHONE FUND £0.00 (spent some on a top up card and need the rest for McDonalds!)

*

So now I am actually thirteen! I am a teenager. And I have a boyfriend! Been thinking about it: now that I'm going out with Tarquin and doing loads of cool things, I'm not going to have time to finish my life story — at least not at the moment anyway. But maybe I could get one of those ghostwriters to help me out? Like celebs do? I'll have to think about it.

Have already been thinking about my future feature in OK! magazine. I think it might go something like this:

The Mum Hunt

Gwyneth Rees

Matthew pulled a scornful face. 'How can you miss someone you've never known?'

Esmie does miss her mum, even though she was only a tiny baby when she died. She has a photo by her bed – and sometimes, when she needs advice or just fancies a chat, she asks her mum for help. Sometimes she even hears her reply.

But Esmie thinks her dad is lonely. And her big brother Matthew would definitely benefit from a female influence. So Esmie decides to take action – she's going to find her dad a girlfriend. Beautiful, clever, charming, kind to children and animals . . . How hard can it be to find the perfect partner for your dad?

MEG CABOT

The PRINCESS DIARIES

What readers said about Meg Cabot's The Princess Diaries

"I love your books *The Princess Diaries*. I need to know how I can contact Amelia Thermopolis. I want to chat with her."

Brandi

"Mia is such an awesome character. All I want to say is keep up the good work so people like me can continue to read your books and dream of being a princess."

Maggie, 13

"You probably think I am nothing like Mia – but it's incredible how when I read the first *Princess Diaries* book, I thought it had been written about me! We're identical – apart from the whole princess thing."

Rachel, 12

"I love *The Princess Diaries* and the movie. I laughed out loud tons of times at it and annoyed my sister."

Lindsay

A selected list of titles available from Macmillan and Pan Books.

The prices shown below are correct at the time of going to press. However, Macmillan Publishers reserve the right to show new retail prices on covers which may differ from those previously advertised.

Meg Cabot		
The Princess Diaries	0330 48205X	£5.99
The Princess Diaries: Take Two	0330 482068	£5.99
The Princess Diaries: Third Time Lucky	0330 482076	£5.99
The Princess Diaries: Mia Goes Fourth	0330 415441	£5.99
The Princess Diaries: Give Me Five	0330 420461	£9.99
Gwyneth Rees		
The Mum Hunt	0330 410121	£4.99
Mum's from Planet Pluto	0330 420410	£9.99
Georgina Byng		
Molly Moon's Incredible Book on Hypnotism	0330 399853	£4.99
Molly Moon Stops the World	0330 990447	£12.99
Ellen Potter		
Olivia Kidney	0330 420836	£7.99
Kate Saunders		
Cat And The Stinkwater War	0330 997719	£9.99

All Pan Macmillan titles can be ordered from our website, www.panmacmillan.com, or from your local bookshop and are available by post from:

Bookpost
PO Box 29, Douglas, Isle of Man IM99 1BQ

Credit cards accepted. For details:
Telephone: 01624 836000
Fax: 01624 670923
E-mail: bookshop@enterprise.net
www.bookpost.co.uk

Free postage and packing in the UK.